CODA

RAJANI KANTH

Published in the United States by
Harvard Square Editions
www.HarvardSquareEditions.org

ISBN: 978-1-941861-11-0

Printed in the United States of America

For My Mother:
Kesavan Kesari

BOOK ONE

THE
JOURNEY

CHAPTER ONE
Black Swan

It had happened.

There was no getting over it.

He didn't remember when it started, or how, or when it stopped, or why.

And here he was – alone.

He didn't know why.

Meaning, why, and how, he had been spared.

His body, though naked, and pasted with dark ash and grime, was oddly clean of abrasions or burns.

The sun was blocked from view now, for a small eternity.

He couldn't count days any more, or weeks.

The stars did not shine.

Vapors, in great, dark clouds, rose everywhere.

Perhaps he was dead.

And it was all a dream.

But he could still feel.

And sense.

He was alive.

In a world that was all dead.

CHAPTER TWO
The Meander

He had been walking for, maybe, a very, very, long time.

But the vista remained ever unchanged.

A pockmarked earth, smoldering, dank, and silent.

Except when a wind, a strange wind, blew - accompanied by a cacophony of motley sounds.

Things blowing about, willy-nilly, clinging, clanking, rustling.

Where was he?

He thought he had amnesia.

Who was he?

Maybe it would come back.

His memory that is.

And if it didn't?

How would he know?

He couldn't answer the queries, but kept walking.

At some point, he must reach someplace.

Maybe the ocean shore.

Maybe the far end of the globe.

Perhaps he was in Australia.

Or was it Africa?

How long had he been walking?

He didn't remember eating, but he had had a drink in a small rivulet of slag.

It was the foulest drink of his life.

Might have been acid, or worse.

Didn't matter, he was thirsty.

He hoped he wouldn't be thirsty again.

The thick, grimy soot that enveloped his body couldn't be brushed off.

It was almost too dark to see except when the off-remnants of burning cinders let off a thin glow here and there.

The cinders were few and far between: how long ago did it all happen?

How was he still alive?

He didn't remember eating.

But he must have, because he felt no hunger.

Nor was he cold, despite his nakedness: the air was warm and humid, and covered him like an all-embracing cloak.

His skin itched, but he had long since ceased to pay any attention to physical discomfort.

He must walk on.

To the ends of the earth, and then on again.

What else could he do?

CHAPTER THREE
Going Maudlin

Mother, father, infant child, he said to himself, over and over, as he walked.

Mother, father, infant child.

That's a family.

He must have had a family.

Maybe he was the father, or maybe the child.

Where were they?

Did they simply evaporate?

Mother, he shouted.

Father, he shouted.

Brother? Oops, he didn't have a brother.

The shouts rang loud, and echoed, only to mix with the wind.

All gone, he shouted, all gone.

He laughed out loud.

Then screamed.

Then he ran like a creature demented, howling all the way.

But it only tired him, so he stopped.

He had been doing this for a long, very long, time.

It didn't change anything.

How many miles had he walked?

Countless, he thought.

He hoped it wasn't Australia.

For then he could walk forever and ever: and never get anyplace.

Maybe, he was on a small island and would soon reach the shore of a welcoming sea.

It was important, he thought, to get to the shore.

The sea may have something big to say, or show.

Or it might just carry him someplace.

No, that was crazy.

The sea would simply swallow him in a trice, like the darkness.

But he still needed to get to it.

The motion of the waves might yet remind him of life.

Or something close.

CHAPTER FOUR
Identity

He tried to sing.

But could not remember any songs.

So he trilled.

La, la, la… but his voice gave up.

I must talk to myself, he said loudly.

Keep talking, boy, he said.

He wondered what his name was.

What language was he thinking in?

How could he guess?

Was he Chinese?

If so, his name might be Yuan.

No, that was the currency.

How about Lao?

Hello, Lao, he shouted, before subsiding.

Or, maybe he was an Eskimo.

He didn't know any Eskimo names.

A mirror.

He needed a mirror to see his face.

Where could he find a mirror?

Keep talking, boy, he said.

And keep walking.

There could be nothing else to do.

He would fall down when sleep overcame him, rise again when he woke - but kept walking.

Motion: that was the key.

Keep moving and talking: two things he could still do.

CHAPTER FIVE

Echoes

I am a man, he said.

I am a man, he shouted.

I live on planet Earth.

It still was planet Earth.

Where were the other planets?

What were they seeing of Earth right now?

Did they know it was gone?

Did they know?

Did they?

Could they?

Darkness at noon, where is the moon?, he yodeled, cupping his hands over his mouth.

It was almost a song - it rhymed.

He kept up the chanting.

Then, of a sudden, he sat down.

He didn't much feel like singing.

Or talking.

He just sat.

Quietly.

Listen, he said to himself, to the sound.

Listen to the sound of nothingness.

Listen to it all, smouldering, smoking.

He could listen, if he still couldn't see.

He could barely feel.

Though he wasn't sure what he felt.

But he could hear.

I have five senses, he thought.

Five, or was it six?

What were they?

He stood up.

It was time to dance.

He did a jig, or something like a jig.

He couldn't be sure.

The world swam around him, as he went round and round.

Blackness above, blackness below.Blackness all round.

He closed his eyes.

Then opened them.

There was not much appreciable difference.

I want to see, he shouted.

I want to see my world.

This is my world.

This is MY world.

The echoes simply came crashing back, as he fell to earth, quite dizzy with the spinning.

CHAPTER SIX

Idea

He remembered, but in bits and pieces.

Or, maybe, he just thought he remembered.

Children singing: or was it birds?

Or both?

Children and birds, singing sweetly.

As the sun shone on them.

The sun.

Ah, that was a relief.

Somewhere, above the thick cloud cover, the sun still shone brightly.

Maybe, even sweetly.

If only.

Wait: he had an idea.

A mountain top.

Yes, not the sea.

The sea would be just another zone of blackness

A mountain-top.

If only he could find one.

Then, he would climb up, and feel the sun shine on him.

Yes.

It had to be done.

It must be done.

It must.

Time to set off for the mountains.

Where were they?

Were they snow-tipped?

Then he could never get up there.

Perhaps they were smaller hills, but just high enough.

The sun.

It had to be found.

The singing. The birds. The children.

He started to shake.

The memory was powerful.

He could feel the sunshine.

He could hear the children.

Could it be?

No, no, no.

No, he shouted.

It could not be.

It could never be.

It could never be.

He said the word a few times.

Never, never, never.

Should he laugh or cry?

It made no difference.

Nobody.

Nothing.

Just him.

Good grief.

CHAPTER SEVEN
The Climb

He set off for the mountains.

North, probably.

How could he figure north?

He didn't know.

A compass. He didn't have one.

So, he followed his nose.

It pointed where it pointed.

Africa had mountains.

So did Australia.

And Asia.

The Americas.

Europe?

No, too cold, too far north.

And he wouldn't have lasted. So, it wasn't Europe.

Brilliant.

I know where I am.

I am not in Europe.

The soil was black with soot and grime and stuff: if he dug deep, he might have a clue.

Or, he might not.

He couldn't dig deep.

No, mountains were by far the better way.

Maybe, if he walked on for days on end.

But, he couldn't tell day from night.

How could he count the days?

Easy:1, 2, 3?

But, seriously, how?

Must keep walking.

Must.

Rise and shine: then walk.

From here to the mountains.

And then, to climb them.

Al the way to the top.

All the way to the top of the world.

The world that was now bereft and bare.

And mantled with darkness.

CHAPTER EIGHT

Questions

It couldn't be.

It just couldn't be what it was.

This was a living Earth.

For Millennia.

So what happened?

A big bang is said to have created it.

Many big bangs now had ended it.

For all living things.

Why?

Where did it all begin?

How far back must one go?

To Wars.

Civil Wars.

Revolutions.

Imperial conflicts.

Building, for hundreds of years.

Building, slowly, for hundreds of years.

Building, surely, for hundreds of years.

Building, building, building…

And then: Boom !

Didn't everyone know?

Some did.

The many didn't.

But he knew.

All along.

He tried, early on, like others, to point.

To identify.

To restrain. To wave a red flag.

But to no avail.

He was nothing.

Not a king.

Nor prime minister.

Nor a president.

Just, and barely, an average Joe.

With a (small) voice.

It was no use.

Powers don't listen to people.

But he tried.

And tried.

And tried.

And he, like others, failed.

Then, he had given up trying.

I failed, he yelled, jumping high, I failed.

We all failed, said his ego, waking.

We failed Us.

And, each other.

And the Planet.

CHAPTER NINE
Planetary

The Planet.

The great big ball of molten hellfire.

The great big ball of fire which spawned life.

It was all too crazy.

How was it possible?

Yet it was.

He could be sure.

He was alive.

Just him - and the Planet.

In the Beginning?

In the End.

Just the Two of them.

What a lot of space.

The oceans.

The plains.

The mountains.

All for him.

For him, alone.

For a while.

He should bend down and kiss the Earth.

The good Earth.

Except, it was grimy and gooey.

And radioactive.

Oh, no.

So he was radioactive, too.

What did it mean?

Was he going to glow in the dark?

He wasn't.

But he was going to die.

Like everyone.

Everybody dies.

But not all at once?

Yes, they did.

All at once.

Almost all at once, as deadly mists swept everywhere.

How did they do it?

What did they let loose?

What Frankenstein toxins had the militaries unleashed?

Who would ever know?

Not him, anyhow.

But, why didn't he die?

He was saved.

For what?

And why?

The Planet.

Maybe the Planet knew something he didn't.

CHAPTER TEN
Motion

He walked on as dark, cloudy, vapors rose, and poured down on, and past, him.

He had long since ceased to notice them.

He was thankful he could walk.

To move is to be alive.

To stop was Unthinkable.

Of a sudden, he had a flash of memory.

Light spread everywhere upon a quiet valley.

He could see it all.

A small cottage amidst big fields.

The harvest was still standing.

He could see himself running through the tall grasses, cutting a deep swathe.

He ran faster and faster, but the fields stretched on forever.

He felt nausea, induced by a gathering claustrophobia.

How could he get past the huge walls of hay, on either side?

He panted heavily.

Then ran even faster, in fear.

But, there was no respite.

Then the memory started to fade.

He was walking now, not running.

And there was no wall of hay, standing tall.

And no light.

Just black vapors, and slimy sod beneath his feet.

His toes squirmed, then lost all sensation.

He was back now, out of the vision.

Into the Vortex of his world.

Walking ever so fast.

To reach the distant mountains.

CHAPTER ELEVEN
Distance

He sat down.

To reach the mountains?

Whew.

Where were they?

A few hundred miles?

A few thousand?

Could he walk that far?

Or, should he just sit where he was.

Or lie down.

And sleep.

He couldn't sit, because the slime rose up sickeningly to his calves.

At least walking lifted you off it, every step.

The slime was the hard part.

Though it was all soft and gooey.

He had always loathed gooey stuff.

Couldn't stand to touch it.

And now the world, like himself, was covered with it.

Except, maybe, the tops of those high mountains.

So he had no choice.

He had to find them.

He rose up.

Time to walk again.

But there was that sensation again, at the pit of his stomach.

He would find the nearest stream, and put his hand down in

the grimy waters.

Eyes closed, he put in his mouth whatever stuck to his hand.

He hoped it was twigs and leaves.

He couldn't tell what it was.

But it eased that pit of the stomach feeling, and he could walk on.

CHAPTER TWELVE
A Plan

He stopped.

There had to be a Plan.

Yes.

He needed to do some reckoning.

He was alone in the world.

How could he be sure?

He was sure.

It was just one of those things.

All alone.

So he could invent his world.

That was it.

He could invent his world now, no one to question him.

It was starting to look easy.

Two hundred miles, he said.

It's two hundred miles to the nearest mountains.

Why?

Because wherever you are, there's some mountains two hundred miles away.

He had just decided that.

So it must be true.

Two hundred miles, he had said, and two hundred it was going to be.

He could walk twenty miles in a day,

So it would take him ten days.

Wow!

Easy as pie.

How could he count the miles?

Easy.

Every step was about a foot.

Three steps to a yard.

1760 yards to a mile.

See, it could be done.

He just had to keep counting the steps.

Presto, he could now figure out the passage of each day.

Twenty miles gave him a day.

He could time the rest of his life, forever.

CHAPTER THIRTEEN

Control

He laughed.

It was the first time he had laughed since…   .

He was getting back in control.

He could reckon Time.

He could reckon distance.

The sky was the limit: if he could but see it.

And once he got to the mountain, the sun would shine on him.

And he would see the heavens.

And the goodly stars at night.

But wait.

The mountains were cold.

Could he endure?

He would have to improvise.

Cover himself with stuff.

Any stuff.

He would find the right stuff along the way.

Yes, he said.

A mile or so before he found the mountains, he would find a forest.

And the forest would give him the stuff he needed.

It was brilliant, really.

Amazing what a little planning could accomplish.

He walked on, jauntily.

There shall be light at the end of the mountain top, he said.

He laughed again at his own wit.

This was not as bad as it looked.

It was getting better all the time.

CHAPTER FOURTEEN
She

There is no one like me.

He remembered saying that to himself, a long, long, long, time ago.

Now there was truly no one like him.

There was No One.

He stopped.

No one.

Once again, the old flashback came flushing in.

The cottage, the meadow, the garners.

And, oh yes: *Her.*

He could not move.

She.

His wife.

He remembered her now, doing dishes.

She always did dishes, no politics intended.

Great, heaping, armfuls of dishes.

And he would watch, very mindfully.

The bracelet on her arm would tinkle lightly as the faucet ran, the plates clashed, and the pots clanked.

He could hear that tinkle now.

The image started to fade.

His wife.

Once upon a time.

The image was gone.

The blackness came rushing in again.

He walked on, less encumbered.

Amnesia had its uses.

CHAPTER FIFTEEN
Myths

The world lived on Myths.

Great, big, mystifying myths.

Some good, some bad, some deadly.

The Powers that incinerated the world had their Great, Big , super, self-justifying Myths.

The people that opposed them had their own little, tiny, myths.

The two fables clashed: as Ideology fought Utopia.

Sort of like the Crusades.

Except, both sides lost.

And all died.

Including bystanders.

He had seen it coming.

He had once tried to draw the attention of all.

Many had, in fact, understood.

But how were they to act?

Nobody knew.

So, one Event led to another.

Then another.

And then: *Kaboom*?

I will not live on myths, he said, softly, reminiscing.

Blackness engulfed him as he walked.

The blackness was not a myth.

He was not a myth.

So he was, sort of, safe: the world had ended: - and its many myths had perished too.

Along with his dear ones.

CHAPTER SIXTEEN
Order

He kept counting his steps.

Feet, yards, miles, gave him days, hours, and minutes.

He was a walking clock.

Every twelve hours he would stop, to sleep.

I am in tune with Circadian rhythms, he thought, of a kind.

I am regular now.

He tried to observe space, between his bizarre meals.

A new Order was developing.

The blackness.

It was now a Habitat.

His habitat.

He must learn to adapt.

Like his ancestors.

Adapt to a lightless world.

Like creatures of the deep.

The forest he would meet, in nine to ten days, would soon be his home.

If it were found burnt to a crisp, like all else: well, he would live in the cinders.

Ashes to ashes.

Memories were his enemies, so Evolution perhaps had quite mindfully erased them.

Without them, he could just about cope.

CHAPTER SEVENTEEN
Recall

He had now walked for eight days, by his clock, barring periods of rest.

The forest had to be close by.

The vistas, however, had not changed.

Charred blackness everywhere.

Dying streams choked with black, grimy, sludge , which furnished his now staple food and drink, crossed his meanderings ever so often.

He walked in rhythm now, humming the count in step with his feet.

He closed his eyes often so that, upon opening them, there could be just the barest semblance of light, in contrast.

But, there was no appreciable difference.

The blood vessels in his eyelids shone bright, in red and yellow flashes.

Like a thousand suns, he sang.

Like a thousand suns.

Suns.

He stopped.

Another memory was breaking in.

Suns.

His son.

Their son.

A little boy, who ran chasing rabbits all day in the fields.

A little boy who chased rabbits.

A little boy.

Try as he might, his name was beyond him.

He smiled.

The vision was generous enough.

He didn't need a name.

His son and his wife, playing in the field.

He walked right up, into the illusion; so real it seemed, that he opened his eyes, then closed them tightly shut again to recapture it.

And stumbled.

It was Day Nine.

And he had just fallen flat, upon some clumps of charred bushes.

His forest.

It was there.

Just as he had calculated.

Naturally.

CHAPTER EIGHTEEN

Ascent

He tugged, and pulled, at the roots, and wrapped the clumps, vines and all, clumsily all around himself, like they were clothes.

He was now covered from head to foot, looking like a small tree himself.

He could climb that mountain now.

No fear.

Just one more day would bring him to the mountain.

The mountain would be, maybe, a mile high.

They usually were.

And he would climb that mile in just so many hours.

Aah.

He sat down in the slush.

He could rest now.

He had earned it.

He was now, sort of, at Base Camp.

He fell fast asleep.

He awoke, and realized he had lost track of time again.

Time only began when he walked.

He could count seconds, of course, but not in his sleep.

Rats.

But wait: there was another way.

He ate only once a day.

So, each time his stomach turned, it was a day past.

And, right now, his stomach was sound.

So, Day Nine hadn't yet gotten done.

CHAPTER NINETEEN
The Boy

His mind was blank.

But, every now and then, a shaft of memory would sear his consciousness, only to leave it blank again.

He couldn't tell if it was really a memory, or if he were simply dreaming.

If it were a dream, he wished he would go on dreaming so he could see color and light and, yes – people.

Dogs. He sat up.

He saw a dog, in his mind's eye, leaping to catch a stick.

Get it, boy, cried a small voice.

Come on, urged another, gentle voice.

That's it. It was their dog, Woof.

A name. Finally, a name!

The dog named Woof: his little boy had named him.

Woof, woof.

Yes. Or, maybe he was mistaken.

But he could see the little family playing out, in the field, in the sun.

He watched, and watched, with eyes closed, until the vision first blurred - and then faded.

He rose.

His stomach stirred.

It was time to head for that mountain.

He had but one whole day to find it.

He started walking again, trying to bring back the Vision.

It wouldn't come back.

CHAPTER TWENTY
Music

The Universe.

And Evolution.

How could he escape thinking?

Life evolved sequentially, but became extinct suddenly.

Surely, it wasn't possible.

Of course not: he was still alive, not dead.

Or was he?

How would he know?

Could this be the Afterlife?

No, he couldn't be alone in the afterlife.

There should be zillions of companions.

Where were they?

Hiding?

Not likely.

So, he was still upon Mother Earth.

Safe and sound.

Sound.

He heard music.

His heart leaped.

Music: he loved music.

He would lie around for hours, listening to it.

There was music playing right now, in his head.

He couldn't identify the scores, but it played all the same.

He walked faster, in time to the racy rhythms.

Should he dance?

He was too weary to dance.

No, he would dance.

He ran, dancing.

But that meant he couldn't keep track of time, so he slowed down again.

The music stopped.

He stopped, too.

This thing about evolution was bothering him.

The evolutionary clock had blown up.

It was Over.

For keeps.

CHAPTER TWENTY-ONE

Hope

He wished he could cry.

But he couldn't.

He tried hard.

Why could he not express grief?

Because shock muffles grief.

Yes.

He was in shock.

I don't know why.

I don't know where I am.

I don't know who I am.

Bit like Adam.

So maybe he was the New Adam.

The Adam who would generate the New World.

The brave new world.

The bad new world.

The barren new world.

Yes, he could regenerate it.

Perhaps there was a way.

To clone himself.

Spiritually.

Planet Earth would help him.

It had to.

It could not let Itself become extinct.

He was the planet now.

And the planet was him.

Whew.

So, he might survive after all.

There was hope.

He jumped to his feet.

Time to walk again.

CHAPTER TWENTY-TWO
Sisyphus

Day 10.

He was there, or close.

In the darkness, he saw strange silhouettes.

Or, so he thought.

Of towering mountains.

He was at their feet now.

The mountains, like step-ladders, would lead him up to the high heavens.

Where he could look above the vapors.

Where he could see.

Brightly and clearly - the *End of the World.*

Or, maybe the Blessed Damozel leaning out of heaven.

He began the weary ascent, heavy of step.

A mile: he had to climb an entire mile to get clear of the mists.

He closed his eyes to count his steps.

They were small, tiny, steps.

The slope was steep.

Climb every mountain.

Ford every sea.

Easier sung, than done.

He tripped more than once, and hurtled down hundreds of feet.

But he simply rose, and started over.

Like Sisyphus.

Yes, the Myth of Sisyphus.

No myth that.

He was living it.

He was surprised his feet hadn't given way.

They were covered with a makeshift shoe-wrap made of creepers and twigs.

He couldn't tell if they were bruised.

Or bleeding.

They were too far away from his mind.

They seemed to have their own volition.

Just as well - for he couldn't tell them what to do.

He was way too tired.

He would sleep whilst they worked away.

Keep climbing, feet.

Pity he had only two - centipedes had the edge in this game.

Maybe they would take over evolution now, if any were left alive.

CHAPTER TWENTY-THREE
Species-Being

He didn't remember *Who* pushed the button.

Maybe they were several.

There were lots of buttons, too.

And they all got pushed.

Naturally: that's why they were there in the first place.

Almost the greatest fireworks display the planet had ever known, since the Big Bang.

People and pyrotechnics – there was a fatal attraction.

And, why not?

We live on a great Ball of Fire, and call it Eden.

So, it had to happen.

Almost like Destiny.

Men - yes, men - just couldn't help it.

It was their *Species-Being*.

What was eerie was the silence that spread everywhere.

The world ended neither with a bang nor a whimper.

Everything was simply snuffed out, without a sound.

Everything, but He.

The Lone Recorder of the Story of Earth.

CHAPTER TWENTY-FOUR
Consciousness

The climbing was tortuous.

Darkness made it hard to reconnoitre.

He had to push on blindly, slipping and falling often.

But, he had no choice.

It had to be done.

He had to make it to the top.

He didn't feel like resting much.

He was well past weariness.

He was past fever and fret.

His own ceaseless motion astounded him.

In all that grime and slime and dark, he alone was restless.

Perhaps, he had expired - and just didn't know.

Maybe this was the After-life.

He couldn't imagine Hell being a big bowl of black jello to wallow in.

And he was the Last - he could not die without the death of evolution.

Nature had a Plan.

It always did.

Except people ignored it, and thought they were superior.

He hadn't.

He always felt one with All Things, animate and inanimate.

He spoke to his car, his house, his dog.

All things were conscious.

Alive.

And splendrous.

And yet all things must pass.

It was too strange.

Nature had a plan: but what was it?

Right now, it appeared that it bore in the direction only of his own immediate extinction.

CHAPTER TWENTY-FIVE

Isms

Men argue.

Men fight.

And matters get 'settled': now this way, now that.

It had been that way for aeons.

And so they were 'settled', one last time.

For keeps.

No scope left for arguments.

No one left to argue, nothing left to argue about.

A perfect solution, one might think.

The world was unified now, in Absence.

Socialism, Capitalism, Any-and-All Isms, all buried once and for all in dank, green, vapors.

Maybe it was nature's Solution to Humankind.

The only species with the capacity to asphyxiate the planet with its own noxious ways.

Except, the planet did not wait that long.

And asphyxiated the species instead, almost literally.

He climbed up the mountain wearily, but determinedly.

CHAPTER TWENTY-SIX
Idylls

He remembered, if in bits and parts.

The tumult.

The strife.

The International Disarray.

The Big Powers covering naked Imperium with Big Lies.

The little ones covering their fear with strident talk.

Everyone with something to hide, or hide from.

The rising cacophony of tough talk and rhetoric.

The inaudible pleadings of the few sane.

But Men, once aroused to passion, will have their Consummation.

Capitalism could not tame Patriarchy: Reason could not dull Emotion.

He had seen it all coming, right in his little mountain village home.

Sitting in the yard, as birds soared overhead, in a clear blue sky, and the dog, in a paroxysm of mock fury, worried a stick.

He could remember his wife, and how he did stare at her.

And she would look over, catching his anxiety, and inquire.

And he would smile, but wanly.

And they would both turn to look at their little boy, agog with the intensity of horseplay, all oblivious of the Crisis building without.

His wife.

Their little boy.

Their dog.

An Idyll from the past, like the world they had inhabited.
And now he must climb to the top of the world.
To ask God why it had all transpired the way it had.

CHAPTER TWENTY-SEVEN

Queries

God.

He sat down on the perilous slope.

He had not thought much about god in all those fiery days.

Is that where the blame lay?

Should he castigate the gods?

Had they failed the Planet?

Or, had they succeeded in removing a scourge?

He had never thought much about god.

Creation was a miracle, of course.

But a miracle was merely that which could not be explained – as yet. So, he was content to wait, to get Answers through critical reflection, through the Sciences that were, apparently, jogging along in leaps and bounds: or, so he had been led to believe.

But Scientists often failed to ask Big Questions.

And left it to other domains to persevere.

Rather than assisting them.

At any rate, his Mission was now clarified.

He would go to the top of the mountain, and challenge the gods to answer.

It would be the Ultimate Question.

At this late stage of devolution, god could hardly fail to answer.

He was possibly the last 'Developed', Inquisitorial, form of life left.

After him, god would quite necessarily have to be silent.

Speak now, or forever hold your peace!

Yeah, god.

CHAPTER TWENTY-EIGHT
Forewarnings

His wife had gone to meetings, councils, and assemblies.

Had marched, fasted, prayed, and picketed.

He had, quite early, after several such joustings, resolutely stayed home.

He had known it was all foredoomed.

Men don't listen to Reason, he had said.

But we must try to make them listen, she had replied.

It has been tried, he said, from Christ to Gandhi.

We have no other choice, she had said.

Yes we do, he had said softly, there is but only One thing to do.

She had looked at him, quizzically.

Stay together, Unto the Last.

And she had shaken her head.

And had left: to carry on the good struggle, full of resolution, energy, zeal , and will.

He knew they might not see each other again, as he stood by the farmyard gate with their son.

An intuition?: he could not be sure.

He saw her disappear down the curving pathway, followed, at a distance, by the barking dog.

Where is mom going?, asked the child, solemnly.

To the far ends of the earth, he had whispered.

He had gone in that evening and thrown out the tv set and the radio.

He did not wish to hear that one Last Big Lie.

The telephone he left hooked on – just in case she…?

He moved his son's bed into his own room.

Even the dog's hamper he set close by.

The days rolled by.

Soon, the mails were not delivered.

The power stalled, though he had his own generator.

He also had stocks of food and gas.

His neighbor's wife came driving up one day, and tooted her horn.

He walked out to the gate.

Their old van was full with family, pets, and odds and ends.

They looked at each other, unable to speak.

You have heard?, the woman had asked, finally.

He had shrugged, non-committally.

You are staying?, she had asked incredulously.

He nodded.

For a long moment, each stared at the other, stupidly, like a bemused cow.

Then, he had , wryly, waved them off, and saw them go hurtling up the country road.

They were off: but where to?

CHAPTER TWENTY-NINE
Night

He could not recall how it happened.

It was Over before he even knew it had started.

Images were warped by shock, trauma, and acute disability.

The only enduring simulacrum was of the Night Perennial, where the sun never rose.

He didn't know how long - days, weeks - he had lain, in a sort of a coma.

His environs were not distinguishable.

And not a soul, far as he knew, existed anywhere.

He had run blindly, in all directions, forever: but there was no respite.

Black vapors, and eerie green light , bathed all things.

The sky was invisible.

The ground covered with ooze.

The air , acrid, smelt of burning things.

His skin, much like his eyes, smarted and itched.

Felt as if his lungs would come bursting out of his mouth.

The distress stifled all emotion.

Yes, he had much to ask of this god when he saw it, face to face, upon that mountain top.

CHAPTER THIRTY
Choices

He had to wonder at his own Choices.

A Force of One, he was not.

He had not marched, or protested, lately: except simply by Evasion.

He knew: and so did not wish to know.

It was more important to secure your hearth when hell was breaking loose, or about to.

He was artist, poet, perhaps even a philosopher - not a politician. Never that.

He had watched hoary political corruption, greed, and lust for power run amok.

Of course thousands, even millions, protested and marched.

But the world belonged to the Powers, not to the populace.

The cancer had run too deep for change – at the top.

So, Another kind of Change would have to cut in.

He knew that Nature would repair her ravages.

But, even he didn't know the extent to which the planet would fight back at those who upset its Balances.

His wife did not believe in such an Apocalypse.

She believed in the inherent goodness of 'people'.

She loved 'humanity'.

And she thought it morally wrong to 'cop-out'.

If everyone thinks like you, humankind would never change, she said.

But everyone wouldn't, he argued: I do what I do, because they do what they do.

But, she didn't really understand.

She was an idealist, perhaps.

And he was the Incorrigible Realist.

Who was right?

It didn't much matter in this instance, of course.

But he was left with nagging moral qualms.

Had he let the planet down?

Worse, had his family perished on account of him?

He would have to live/die with that burdensome load over him.

Yes, he had much to query this god with.

He hoped it did live up there, high on the mountain top.

Hiding from the world it had just Uncreated.

No one else who could help atone for his guilt.

CHAPTER THIRTY-ONE
Darkness

Let there be light.

He had now lived without it, and didn't remember it at all any more as a sensory phenomenon,

Instead, it was a concept, a mere idea of brightness.

All he could 'see' was primal slime and darkness, like being on the ocean floor too deep for rays to penetrate.

Any more of this, and he might grow fins, and 'swim' in that mushy ether.

Ever so often, his heart would drop at fear that this darkness may never go away.

That he would never reach the mountain top.

That he would never see the health-giving sun, or the night stars, and the pale ivory of the serried moon.

How could it be?

His was of a species that had journeyed ambitiously to the far planets.

Seeking alas, only to plunder, colonise.

And here he was clamoring, merely to climb a hill.

A feat fit for a mountain goat.

And within the lights of the lowliest Sherpa.

He trekked on relentlessly, heart pounding, chest heaving.

It seemed to get only steeper as he climbed.

Like the North Face of Everest.

He felt, he fancied, a drop in temperature, unless it was merely the wind glancing off his own perspiration.

He was covered in vines and leaves.

Enough insulation, he hoped.

Besides, there was no snow, so he wasn't anywhere in the Himalayas, or the Alps.

So, chances were he wouldn't freeze to death.

But, he might have wished he could have carried a torch.

To light the way.

So he didn't feel he was blind.

CHAPTER THIRTY-TWO
Vertigo

Should he keep a log?

But how?

And Who, there, left to read it?

Visitors from another planet, light years from now?

Here he was with the Greatest Story ever to tell, but no one to tell it to.

Except Martians.

He clutched the face of the mountain as he climbed, now and then, out of a severe feeling of vertigo.

It must be very steep indeed.

And harshly rocky.

His head swam, as he climbed, and he felt dizzy.

He felt a gnawing in the pit of his stomach, but he was not willing to stop.

Besides, there was no vegetation here he could eat.

And he was fearful of falling off the mountainside into, who knows, what gorges below.

How many days had he climbed?

He had lost count, out of sheer fatigue.

Of course he could figure things, if he had the energy to.

A mile high would this mountain be, to be sure.

So he could, with due reckoning, estimate time remaining, if not energy remaining.

When had he last eaten?

Or drank?

He didn't remember.

Did it matter?

Maybe, he had mutated - and didn't need to eat any more?

Man, without Hunger, would be a different animal indeed.

A more pacific one, he hoped, but different for sure.

Less likely to enslave, or be enslaved?

But, there was no telling.

Other animals, generally, kill to eat: men kill for reasons unfathomable, and/or non-existent.

So, even as a mutant, there was not much, real evolutionary hope.

Of course, he could keep a log: a tell-tale mark on the hillside, etched with tree limbs, to tell of his epic journey to the top of the world.

But it was no use: like tracks in the sand, they would perish almost instantly.

So he climbed, and climbed , and climbed.

Soon, for the umpteenth time, his legs gave way, and he sank to the ground dully to rest, eyes closing involuntarily.

Before he fell asleep, he was conscious of but a fraction of a dim fear of falling off the hillside, thousands of feet below, if he lost his tenuous hand and footholds.

CHAPTER THIRTY-THREE
Shame

Was it shame or guilt, he couldn't tell, but he dreamed of both
- if it were a dream.

Interesting difference.

Shame involved *Others*, a loss of face.

Guilt was a private, personal thing.

He could never have any shame any more.

But the guilt he would carry to his grave.

We are given the capacity to save the world, he dreamed.

It is nature's plan to vest all with that all-powerful Power.

Even if one were only a force of one.

But he had not felt that force.

Truth be told, he had not wished to save the world, even his
own.

There was a sort of an inner shame.

He was ashamed, in front of his unknown gods, to be part of
the ever so stupid/ignorant genus of *Homo Sapiens*.

What an oxymoron that term was!

Destroying its own world as it had, steadily, for so very long –
and for petty, pathetic, mindless reasons.

He was quite completely nauseated.

There was no decent Exit.

All Men were marred by the same corruption.

The Women bore no guilt, they were beyond the pale of abject
masculinity.

Women built the world, repeatedly: Men destroyed it.

That had been the Saga of Creation.

But why?

Why should that one squalid One-Act Play be repeated endlessly?

Maybe, god was a woman testing the humanity of men.

Christ, like the Buddha, were possibly female Saviors, in male garb.

But the lesson of Love, surely, was wasted on men.

They might have known that.

So, he had accepted Armageddon as inevitable.

As Judgment Day.

It could not be averted.

He dreamt of guilt and shame, as he lay clutching the earth about him.

CHAPTER THIRTY-FOUR
Guilt

He awoke in a foul fever.

Trying to rise too quickly, he lost his hold on the steep face of the mountain.

And he fell now: bouncing off crags and ledges, like a beach ball, torn by sharp rocks, and scoured by jagged tree limbs.

He could not utter a cry, but fell silently, as the makeshift arboreal armor gouged him, in turn, even as the rocky face of the mountain scorched his body in a fierce, fire-like friction.

It was all a whirl.

He closed his eyes, no better though in consequence.

Eyes closed, he could pretend it was a dream.

I am dreaming, he said to himself hopefully, but it was wholly unconvincing.

I am falling, said his senses, in calm retort, falling down to the very bottom.

Eventually, the rocking and rolling and bumping was over: and he was still again, held back from the very edge of a deep, sharply defined, ravine by a solitary tree stump.

He opened his eyes.

He was near close to where he had begun climbing.

He lay in a stupor, unwilling to budge.

Maybe he was paralysed, he thought.

But the thought gave him no special discomfort.

Maybe it was how it was supposed to end.

At the foot of a great mountain, broken and bleeding, bereft of will.

It seemed appropriate.

Strange, what guilt can do.

CHAPTER THIRTY-FIVE
Thorns

Hours, maybe days, he lay unstirred.

The pain had become dull, so he felt it not.

There was a certain peace to this posture of prone stillness.

It was almost soothing.

He waited patiently to be overcome by death.

But the Respite did not come.

Instead, he felt restless.

The peace was out of place.

He had no right to euphoria, even in near-death.

It was no way to allay his guilt.

So he struggled to move again.

Excruciating pain racked his body, but he felt cheered.

This was more the punishment he deserved.

For falling short.

For being apathetic.

For being, ultimately, an egoistic hominid.

And for a million other little acts of omission and commission that had littered his mundane life.

He rose to his feet with his canopy of vines clinging to him in mortal embrace.

He made no effort to disentangle.

This was his own, personal, Crown of Thorns.

He would Endure.

He looked up at the mountain-side again.

He could not see beyond a few feet, for the thick, dark mantle of vapors that surrounded it.

There was no choice.

He had to climb again.

Start Over.

Redeem himself.

That's what they had all missed about the myth of Sisyphus.

That it was all, despite its arduous nature, supremely *Redemptive*.

CHAPTER THIRTY-SIX
Delusion

What did we know, as humans?

About anything?

Nothing.

We knew not who we were, whence we originate, whither we go.

And yet the Human Ego had found its own ways to transcend this lapidary ignorance.

So we made up Colossal Myths.

Super-colossal myths.

Of Origins , Life, and Extinction.

How supremely seductive these fables were!

More so when they were encapsulated in great big monuments of marble and stone, our churches, temples, and prayer halls that seemed to display, arrogantly, boldly, confidently, their claims of intimate knowledge of the universe.

This seamless universe.

This universe without knowable beginning or end.

This fiery ball of imminent havoc, and sudden devastation, we call, blessedly, the good earth.

How deluded can we get?

How can we deceive ourselves so?

Prophets, soothsayers, and seers, vented their rank ignorance in paroxysms of illimitably impossible rhetoric.

And the populace swayed with the weighty words, as if their souls were being tuned to high perfection.

As if they had found a stairway to heaven, maybe to god itself in the goodly Litany of Praise.

But all paths were the same – *they led Nowhere*, except the certainty of mortal extinction.

One by one, we fall to earth, no more wise than we entered.

For all the Good Books, and high sermons.

The priests and the choirboys would all, sooner or later, lie down to sleep forever, returned to primal silence.

Help me, god, he said, as he climbed, wearily.

Not to see you, or even know the truth.

But just to put aside the myths of my own making.

Anthropic allegories, hominid Fantasies.

The lies with which we live our lives, every day.

That was not much to ask.

Of the Supreme Being.

After all, after him, there would be, could be, no more questioning.

He did not wish to know the truth: only to be free of Error.

CHAPTER THIRTY-SEVEN
Atoning

The proper study of mankind is Man?

He climbed with renewed energy, reminded of the Labors of Hercules.

He was ready to labor now, even unto his last breath.

It was Atonement.

For not just his errors, but the delusions of humankind.

For the abject, unspeakable, Tyrannies of (Big) Men.

For the silently borne injuries of women, children, animals, and Lesser Men.

With every step, he would wash away each warm, solitary , tear shed by grieving humankind for millennia.

With every step, he would redeem the species, and beg pardon for their crimes.

With each step, he would ask a blessing for victims and victimizers, alike.

His Role, if it was that, was now looming apparent.

This was why he had not perished.

He was left alive to feel all pains, absorb all grief, and redeem the gnawing despair of the sheer lack of meaning of human existence.

He took bolder steps, applying far less caution.

Now, it didn't matter if he fell, or how often he fell.

He felt Free in his motion.

He shed his canopy, feeling light and airy in his New Mission.

Oddly, his footholds, for all the wanton abandonment of

caution, were as solid as before - if not more.

He was scaling the mountain like a spider runs up a sheer wall, lightly and swiftly.

He could scarce believe his own agility.

Crags, rocks, and promontories, seemed to step aside for him, as he leapt over chasms, tree stumps, and dried-up water springs.

The top of the mountain could not be far at this rate.

But it didn't matter now whether he made it all the way up or not.

He had no need for that grand *tete-a-tete* with god, only his own inner voice.

The dank, vapory, mists seemed vested with more color now, taking on ever changing hues.

He fancied each color change paralleled his own varying exultations of spirit.

The Clouds of Delusion.

They could look awfully pretty at times.

CHAPTER THIRTY-EIGHT
Maya

Maya.

It was a word, a concept, of the ancients

He had read about it, as he had read about much, in his own desultory way.

The world is real, but is also an illusion.

A real illusion one might say.

An illusion created possibly for the Entertainment of the Creator.

No, that was *Leela*, another Eastern concept.

A species of play, pantomime, and parody.

It was not that the Author of the Universe was a glib Post-Modernist: it was that the nature of the universe itself had such beguiling attributes.

He remembered an instance.

He had dropped his key-ring, purely by accident, in the car.

It fell within a single square foot of visible space.

Yet, in that miniscule area, it had, quite simply, vanished.

He had searched for hours on end, to no avail.

The next day, after he had ordered a replacement at high cost, he looked down: and there it lay, gleaming wryly in all of its dull copper tone, almost with a smile upon its face.

That was a bit of Leela.

Those keys knew what they were doing.

Yes, it was a Self-Aware Universe.

That's pretty much how he had known that it was all over,

even before it was.

And why he had gone into a private huddle without troubling to help, in his own miniscule way, to change the world, or try and alter where it was, quite surely, heading.

The universe speaks through us, to us.

It acts through us, for us.

So he had been allowed to live, for reasons best known to the planet.

But he would choose *how* to live: that much was now quite up to him alone.

How many degrees of freedom were there to Free Will?

CHAPTER THIRTY-NINE
Balance

There was a certain lightness to Being.

And a heavier weight to Becoming.

And a really prohibitive bar to Doing.

But he was in motion now, and could not rest.

Up, up, and away, up the steep mountain top, climbing with the dexterity of a nimble mountain goat.

I climb up to the lone founts of my own ego, said a voice.

I climb to reach for a vision of god, said another.

I climb and know not why, said a third.

He disdained all the voices: he had no need to know why.

He was not aiming to fathom meaning.

He was acting out the only Karma left him.

To suffer, to do penance, for all that had been.

To recompense all who had suffered.

To repossess, for them, all they had lost.

To die, ultimately, for all whose varied griefs had been ignored by an apparently uncaring, impotent universe.

There are great Cycles to evolution, Metacycles, even Epicycles.

There are long-drawn curves of learning, forgiveness, and redemption.

The planet allowed enormous free-play, and then pulled back, periodically, of a sudden, catastrophically.

Great eras of rank creativity followed equally great dives into dire destruction.

The Law of Balance that equips all things seemed to illustrate that.

The doom he had experienced around him was written.

The warning signs had lain visible, within reach:of All.

Ignored long enough, they brought forth the Cataclysm

The Resurrection, and the Renaissance, would now have to follow.

Creation had spared him perhaps to chronicle the passage from one order to another.

He was at the origin of the Next Universe, the very next round of evolution.

As he climbed, he was now possessed of great urgency.

He must get there, in time, for the very next Big Bang.

He had to beat god to that climactic cloudburst.

CHAPTER FORTY

Karma

What was god, then, given the immanent dialectic of karma, of causality, of action and reaction, that informed the known universe?

It is not this, it is not that, it is not something else.

It is - and it isn't.

Bit like the mountain he was climbing.

It was there, and it wasn't there.

But together, him and the mountain, formed a necessary dyad: he existed for the mountain, and the mountain existed for him.

Each Affirmed the Other, real or not.

Even if it seemed he was getting the short end of things.

He stopped climbing and sat down, of a sudden, on a precipitous ledge that seemed to lean on the very edge of nowhere.

There could be no fear anymore.

He could jump off the crag if he chose.

The Net Energy of the universe would not have changed.

No, death was merely a minor, micro, rearrangement of energy.

That's all he was now, an energy-form, about ready to mutate.

It didn't matter into what.

CHAPTER FORTY-ONE
Fear

We live in Fear.

It is a dominant species-instinct, an enabling defense against both random and programmed violence from humans, animals, and nature - and the dour premonition of the inevitability of death.

It is the conditioning ether of all our interactions.

Part of civilization is a certain, qualified, reduction of that fear.

He thought of his own fearlessness now.

It was not the way he had lived.

It was not the way the Modern world was constructed.

In fact, Modernism heightened all fears, rational and irrational.

As a child, the very idea of a nuclear bomb had terrified him.

The mushroom cloud at Nagasaki.

He knew then of its reality, of its finality, if not its inevitability.

The Bomb had , for long, set the limit to human, and other ancillary, evolution

Its very existence had set off another kind of a bomb: a Time bomb.

It ticked on relentlessly, with only one event to halt it.

People in power spoke glibly of human rationality, caution, and care.

But he had never bought it for an instant.

No weapon ever made that does not get used, and often.

Except nuclear devices may not be used often.

Without being Self-Limiting.

Each bomb added to the arsenal of humankind ensured the

certainty of Armageddon.

He tried to explain that to his wife, who only shook her head.

Humans can and must stop the madness, she had said.

It is unstoppable, he had replied.

I must go, she had said.

Wish you would stay, he had said, more mildly.

I'll be back, she said.

Time is short, he had whispered.

And she had left.

Only days before the skies burst.

CHAPTER FORTY-TWO
Mammals

We are animals.

Better still, Mammals.

We are vested with species-characteristics which we share with other hominids.

This limits any notion of our being the supernal Masters of the Universe.

If we are made in god's image, then god, too, is an ape.

Jesus was a monkey, as was Siddhartha.

So it is all way less lofty than our delusions would have it.

Our capacity for Sublimation is another Infinite that knows no limit.

We have invented humanity - and humanism.

Elegant Ways, grandiloquent Words.

Social graces, and high etiquette.

Hoping it would conceal our, somewhat pathetic, animal traits.

The bile, the blood, and the mucus.

It almost did work, lifting us far above our desserts.

But, underneath, the grim ape lived on.

We thump our chests, growl, bay, and roar, like lords of the jungle.

The Male Hominids, that is.

And we have made War, and committed mass-murder, at the slightest provocation - or even without it.

But the humanists were not altogether wrong.

Only in one important regard,were we singularly different from animals.

Our appetites, unlike other hominids, know no limits.

CHAPTER FORTY-THREE
From Above

He looked at the mountainside.

It was steep, raw, and unprepossessing.

Face to mountain face, it was altogether bare, rugged, and daunting.

Just a mass of earth and stone, standing up straight instead of lying down flat.

The view from below had been quite different.

He wondered what it would be like to view it all from the top.

If he could ever make it all the way up.

He had no fear now, but that is not to say he had much enthusiasm.

He had never wished to make it to the top - of anything, really.

For any reason.

The view from the top was a tempting notion, still.

From there, you could, maybe, see forever.

From below, generally, one gets another view.

The people at the top knew One Reality.

At the bottom, Another.

And in the middle: it was sort of a No-Man's Land.

Fear of below, Envy of above.

That was the Middle Condition.

He was now, he thought, half-way up.

Why not just park there, and wait for the universe to illumine him one day?

Perhaps the clouds would fade, the vapors evanesce, and the mists clear.

What would he see then?

From his solo perch in the middle?

God?

He knew why so many ancients believed their gods lived high on the top of mountains.

They hoped earnestly that this god-being could see further than their own kings and queens.

Know more, be wiser.

Maybe, even a tad kinder.

He was less sure.

The view from below was necessarily skewed.

It wished too much of the Summit.

It had to believe Virtue was some high-up thing.

That's why we look up, almost instinctively, to the 'heavens'.

But there is no Up or Down, really.

The universe, like a perfect puzzle, is a Circle.

All our wanderings, and wonderings, bring us back to Ourselves.

So, what should he do?

Climb.

Stay.

Or, slide down?

CHAPTER FORTY-FOUR
Ambition

He had no ambition, everyone said.

True, at one level.

But grotesquely untrue at another.

His ambition, truly, overreached them all.

He wished to know.

Not just this or that, but Everything.

So, yes, he was not ambitious.

But he was, too.

There are men who would be kings, and people called that ambition.

But others who wish for even more: to be gods.

No special word for that, unless it was insanity.

She had liked him because he had no ambition.

But was also uneasy, because she knew why.

He was neither the man at the Top, the man at the Bottom, nor the man in the Middle.

But the One who stands apart from the mountain.

She belonged to the foothills, always looking up.

Ideals, Hope, and Faith.

It helped radiate a special energy.

She had no need to climb the mountain, and see it all.

She, too, had no ambition - but was full, instead, of zeal: Plans of Action.

Programs.

Agendas.

It is the ever abundant Utopia of the Powerless.

CHAPTER FORTY-FIVE

Heat and Light

He returned to climbing.

With no particular motivation.

What else could he do?

If he were to die, it wouldn't matter where.

But to live might occasion that effort.

In a dark world, one must seek the light.

Not because light is, always, illuminating, or uncovering.

Indeed light concealed much, like the dark.

Daylight hid clean from view, at its brightest, a myriad galaxies.

So it was not for any great enlightenment that he strove.

But to satisfy himself that he had missed nothing of great import.

That he was alive.

That he was not like the many creatures of the slime who wallowed, apparently blissfully, in a lightless world.

That he needed to feel the sun, to warm his face.

That he was a mammal - and sought heat, and shunned the cold.

That he really couldn't be doing anything else.

CHAPTER FORTY-SIX
Order

Many lived their lives like that.

Not knowing, or thinking.

But doing, day after day.

Without awareness, choice, or freedom.

It were only monotonous, were it not also deadly.

But the human (Man) is a routinized animal that accepts Order.

Even at high cost.

That is how Fascism and Dictatorship survive.

Order and predictability are as important as food and shelter: they are, indeed, and in fact, metaphysical predicates of the same.

The Men who blew up the world, likely believed in their cause.

They felt they had no choice.

They accepted the constraint of 'reality'.

They acted, they felt, rationally.

Anything short would have been irresponsible.

Extraordinary Evil, *per se*, is rare amongst humans (Men) and easily detected.

But mundane reality turns into it, in context of fierce attachment to ideals, norms, and values.

Virtue, when threatened, is ever ready to kill.

Much like Vice.

Except it is a million times more effective, and feels a whole lot more empowered.

Virtue is far bolder than vice.

Virtue and vice are both, in the final analysis, deadly to the human spirit.

To the Mammalian Essence.

To our Species-Being.

CHAPTER FORTY-SEVEN

Reverie

He felt a besotting emptiness.

Not the obvious emptiness around, but an emptiness Within.

He could not name this new emotion, because it was new.

He couldn't fathom it.

It seemed disabling.

He wanted to, suddenly, sit down.

Even on that perilous crag.

But he ignored the powerful urge.

He still had some semblance of Will, even if it had now become pointless, if not exactly dysfunctional.

Climb, he urged himself, and ignore all else.

He started up again, but stopped.

The urging was strong. He leant against the mountain face.

He found himself remembering, as if in reverie.

He was a child again, sporting by the sea.

It was a white, sandy, beach - and the sunlight spread over it like honey on toast.

The sea roared, and billowed, in great big frothing waves, but he had his back turned to it, and was digging away in the sand, building a great big Castle complete with dungeons and moats.

At a distance, other children played, and a few adults were taking a walk quite far away.

The ever ominous noise of the sea, and the fierce, torrid gusts of wind , quite drowned all other noises.

Easy to fall into a reverie on a beach, with the sea, our primal matrix, right by us.

The sun, the feel of sand between your toes, and the vast unscalable dimension of the ocean, lent a stupefaction to all things that simply dwindled in significance, by comparison.

He was busy scooping up sand with his hands, cupping it, and adding it to the architecture already in place.

All others on the beach melted away, as in a long, glancing camera shot.

Suddenly, he had been hoisted high upon a rogue wave that tossed him clear out to sea.

The sun was starting to set, and the tide was pulling out.

He was helplessly flat on his back, floundering on the waves, as strong currents towed him away.

He saw the beach recede, but could not bring himself to shout. Fear and shock quite paralyzed him.

There were no thoughts in his head at all.

Not a soul on the beach had noticed.

His own escorts were walking apace, still far away, quite unknowing.

He was some sixty yards out, soundless, and devoid of all being, when he felt a sudden, opposite thrust; and, seconds later, was thrown back, savagely, right upon the sand castle that was by now nearly submerged in water.

He looked around, and staggered to his feet, stunned by the severity of impact.

The sea was receding now, taking much flotsam and jetsam with it.

Without a word, he raced away from the ocean, as fast as his legs could carry him, all the way home, a mile or so away, without once looking back or stopping. He was feeling the same emptiness now he had felt back then.

CHAPTER FORTY-EIGHT
Memory

In the great Saragossa of the Mind, there is a peculiar place for Memory.

Memory is the organism's defense armor.

It keeps every wound green and alive, so we learn.

But it has limits.

Too much grief, or stress, can delete it.

He could remember discrete events, but they did not quite add up.

It was like knowing a dozen scenes from a movie intimately - but being unable to figure which movie it was, or what the story was about.

He could hardly stand the syncopation of events, processes, and the feelings they evoked.

His own story was fragmented.

His wife, he remembered.

His childhood, too, in that flash of images just recounted.

But there was more.

And he grappled hard to find it.

Then, there was that mountain.

Daunting, steep, tall, and unyielding.

There was a definite connection between the climbing and the remembering.

He wasn't sure how it all worked.

He put all his energy into the climb.

The remembrance could wait.

Rocks and crags , and stony slopes, he negotiated without difficulty, barefooted.

The nettles and bushes that rubbed against him bore him no pain.

Indeed, he felt nothing even as cuts, bruises , and gashes, marked his naked body continuously.

It is the mind that feels pain, not the body.

And his mind was now preoccupied, unobserved by him, with rooting out his memory cells.

Memory is not really deletable, it simply goes into a sort of hibernation.

It takes a species of electrical shocks to wake it up.

Such shocks can be externally, or internally, inspired, and can work either way: of stoking revival, or inducing sleep.

I must climb, his conscious mind said, as he fought his way up, foot by perilous foot.

I must find, said his reactive mind - quite ignoring his resolve.

CHAPTER FORTY-NINE
Yesterday

Up the rocky staircase, he misjudged his footing, and slipped a few feet down, scraping against bare rock.

This time he felt the pain.

It was scorching.

He found sudden, unexpected, rest on a promontory of rock, bush, and nettles, that broke his fall.

He made no attempt to rise again.

He had remembered.

He clung hard to the bush, to feel some comfort, but the bush failed him, stinging him , instead,with its thorny concord.

It was the Night Before.

The evening had been warm.

And he had leaned for hours, after dinner, on the farm fence, staring at the meadow that lay behind, bathed in the glow of eventide.

He turned to see his son rolling on the grass, with their sheepdog, in squeals of laughter, as the dog licked and pawed him.

The quiet meadow, the noisy vignette of childhood: how could such things subsist in the same world as what was taking place in the somber Capitals of the Globe, just then?

His son jumped up to his feet, and ran toward him.

Will you read to me, dad?

He had smiled: of course, he would.

They had gone in, as the light outside was still fading.

He lit the oil lamp he had by the bedside.

What could he read?

He looked at the shelf.

The Invisible Man, The War of the Worlds, the Mill on the Floss.

Old classics that had regaled his own childhood.

He picked up the last.

His son was quite asleep, but he had kept on with the recitation of the melodrama of poor Tom and Maggie.

It had seemed appropriate.

He himself had fallen asleep, on that old rocking chair, open book in his lap, the dog curled up by his feet.

Only one of them would rise from their conjoint sleep.

He clutched the bush even harder, even as the thorns bore deep into his flesh.

There was no respite.

His vision turned even murkier than before, eyes semi-closed and moist.

It was the first time he had come close to tears, since...

CHAPTER FIFTY
The Will

Memory is personal, but consciousness is collective.

He was, unawares, cut off now from the Universal Mind from which living things draw daily sustenance.

His mind was now stripped of its victuals of sustenance.

It had to improvise, find its own inspiration.

Earth, Wind, and Fire there was enough of - but not living, breathing, beholding, life.

But, whence the source?

All he had was bits of memory from which he could extrapolate.

It wasn't enough.

He was rapidly being stripped of his mind.

Left only with Will.

With the energy-force given to all life forms.

Slowly, he rose again and surveyed his world.

The dark form of the mountain face was right by him.

Below, the grey-green mists quite enveloped everything.

Above, even darker clouds blocked vision.

So, he could only view the few feet of space the mountain allowed.

It was enough.

He could still breathe.

The below was his forgotten Past.

The above, his unknown Future.

The spot he stood on, his ever-present Present - his one

certainty other than himself, that always moved with him.

Like a loyal dog.

He geared up his energies.

His mammalian will, his hominidian determination.

And he started to climb across the traverse again, heedless of physical distress.

CHAPTER FIFTY-ONE
Hominids

Hominids need only to breathe.

All else is residual, if often necessary.

Hominids have species-characteristics that thrive in collectivities.

Left alone, they collapse into an asocial, primal state.

He climbed now like an ape, set of purpose, unmindful of hazard.

Fear, other than instinct, did not exist for him.

Only memory connected him to the past, to the known universe.

But the memories failed to add up to anything coherent.

Or, meaningful.

Yet, now he had the blessing of certainty.

He knew he could climb all the way.

He knew he could reach the top.

He was one with his purpose.

The vapors had to be escaped.

And, there was no other place he could be free of the contagion.

Much like a roach knows where to hide, when residents in homes pose threats to its existence.

CHAPTER FIFTY-TWO
Little Things

How far was he from the top?

It didn't matter.

It was not an issue.

How many days would it take to climb?

That didn't count either.

He had not eaten for many days, but felt it not.

He had drank from a little, murky, spring bed - and it was enough.

When he was exhausted, he would simply lean against the face of the mountain, and rest.

Until it was time to move again.

He was leaning thus, when he dreamt again.

It was a woman bending over him, applying a poultice to his arm.

He appeared but a child in the dream.

So the woman was either his mother or a nurse.

He couldn't be sure, since he didn't see her face.

But he could hear her words, whispered softly.

They were soothing.

He could not decipher what she was saying.

But it didn't matter.

It was the quality in the voice that sufficed.

He awoke with a jolt, and tried to bring the dream back by force - but it had vanished.

However, the whisper still echoed in his ears.

He tried to sit instead of standing.

The voice had, somehow, relaxed him.

The hominid world is made of little, not big things.

A touch, a whisper, a light in the eye, other than breath, suffice to make of the world a complete home.

In the filmy darkness, he felt now almost at home.

He was adapting.

It is what hominids do best.

It is why they survived as long as they did.

But, no species lasts forever.

On average, a species subsists about a hundred thousand years, and thence is gone.

And so it was now with hominids, except for him.

The Other apes who ruled this planet for millennia were all gone the way of evolution.

CHAPTER FIFTY-THREE
The Ape

For many unrecorded moons, he kept up the incessant climbing.

This mountain went up forever, like the beanstalks in the old fairy-tale.

The pathway never altered.

The same rocks, the same bushes, the same steep wall.

But, he would not tire.

He thought, at times, of what lay beyond - and above.

What beauteous scene? What ambient light? What manner of heavens?

He remembered starlight, and the splendorous ivory streams that flowed from the moon on dark nights.

He thought of bright sunlight, and the balmy rays that drove flies mad at noon-time.

His animal heart craved these images.

They made him get to his feet and commence labors in great anticipation.

Other memories were less inspiring, and made his journey heavier.

He dreamt of his wife once, and woke up in distress.

She was calling him: but from where?

He could scarce go on that day.

But each vision erased the other, so nothing endured very long.

And, each time, he returned to his new state of highly sentient, but all but unreflecting, being.

He could feel, but could not think.

The absence of fear was quite elational.

Like animals now, he did not know death.

That final quietus he had quite forgotten.

But he knew loss, or the memory of it.

He was using all his limbs now: there was no other way to climb.

On all fours, like the ape he was, he lumbered.

When his feelings got the better of him, he let out loud yells that echoed all around him.

Every now and then, still on all fours, he would look down gingerly, but could see nothing.

There was but one direction to go.

Occasionally, he tried to draw tracks on the mountain side, with a reed or a branch.

Sometimes, he would amuse himself by tossing branches in the air, and catching them with his feet, lying flat on his back in some crevice on the hillside.

He could think, but only in discrete, not continuous, terms, and in pictures.

He would make moan, at intervals, long deep moans that seemed involuntarily to emanate from deep within.

Each time he looked down, he scrambled to climb again, in a hurry, as if afraid of what he saw, though he could see nothing.

He was human in his dreams alone, where some recall was given him.

Waking, he was now but an ape.

CHAPTER FIFTY-FOUR
Fantasies

Life, in some conceptions, is a dream-state.

Or, even a dream within a dream.

What humans project as reality is their own palette of dreams, good or bad.

The Bomb was one such dream.

A Fantasy.

A Genocidal allegory of Male Violence.

But, it took modernist sorcery and witchcraft, *i.e., Science*, to bring it into being.

But dreams, being dreams, need not always be lethal.

There could also be dreams of peace and plenty, like that of Christian evangelists, or Socialists.

Or just plain Peace, minus the plenty, like Buddhists, or Hindus.

And, much like the bomb, once dreamed ,they can be made effectual.

Except dreams don't last forever, good or bad.

The propensity to dream is an Anthropic trait, built into our natures.

What function it serves in Nature's larger plan, is far from clear.

But it is another form of sublimation.

Of seeing things other than how they exist.

It is an odd capacity.

So, a flesh and blood female human can be seen as a madonna, or a porno queen, in male fantasies.

Invested with men's own ideas, and ideals, for better or for worse.

But, it could also be helpful at times.

Hope, for example, is yet another human fancy.

Given, as someone has said, as a sop to the hopeless.

But what a balm to the suffering, and the helpless!

We are given to sublimation simply to survive the unsurvivable.

And yet, surprisingly, Courage, the child of hope, is often able to surmount the very fear that hope was designed to obscure.

It is a world of Paradox.

What could be more paradoxical than the human animal?

Created half to rise, and half to fall, as the poet has it.

Builds to destroy, and destroys to build.

Loves to fight, and fights to love.

And so on.

Faith was another odd commodity.

People believed in gods they had never seen or heard - fought for them, died for them: even , dubiously, lived by their assumed fiats.

They did the same for ideals and beliefs.

Faith in god was just another idea/ideal.

Did gods create people?

Maybe not, as often, as people create gods.

CHAPTER FIFTY-FIVE
Instinct

Our Hero was now quite incapable of such speculation, unless the odd dream brought memory floating back for a brief spell.

He had already mutated, in a way - returned to some antic, primal nature.

The mountain was not an obstacle anymore, nor a means to an end.

It was his natural habitat now.

He would still go to the top, only to secure the fullness of the opportunity it gave him.

He didn't really know why.

Instinct was driving him, not resolve.

He had forgotten about his dialog with God.

He had forgotten the series of events that had him seeking the shelter of the mountain in the first place.

The mind had been replaced with instinct.

But instinct is only the collective memory of a species.

In him lay the Unconfigured Experience of all hominids.

You might say that he was now, unselfconsciously, the wisest ape who ever lived.

The dreams would still come, returning and repeating.

Oft-times, he would wake within his former self, which was highly disorienting.

More often, he would see the dream as we would a film in a foreign language: vaguely familiar it might be, but we really don't know what's being said, or what's going on.

He was a strange dual - part human, part hominid, part cell-bank of all life forms on the planet not yet destroyed.

It was , all in all, quite a heavy rap: though he didn't know it in quite those terms.

CHAPTER FIFTY-SIX
Why Anything?

Who are we?

Where do we come from?

The mundane life snuffs such questions out altogether.

The religious life provides catch-as-catch can answers designed for the consumption of the fearful, and/or the feeble-minded.

To the thoughtful, such queries demand lifelong probes.

In his own life, he had probed and probed - until his mind just gave up.

There were questions that simply had no Answer.

Why life, why death?

Why, indeed, Anything?

Knowledge of our own pitiable ignorance in such areas is another distinguishing characteristic of us, distinct from our fellow mammals.

Knowledge of the certainty of death is the other.

As a Near-Hominid now, he was free of such burdens.

His mind ceased to be a critical drain upon his energies, but functioned instead as a laser beam /radar screen affording him 24/7 protection.

He ate the bark and brambles, much as he could scavenge and scour, now with relish.

The mountain, far from being the challenge it was, was now, simply, home.

Even the vapors, though vexatious, were not unduly threatening.

Occasionally, he actually pondered the idea of descending

down into the depths again.

The slime and the grime did not appear to trouble him.

But some sense of his own incompleteness was an issue.

He climbed now also in search.

In search of his kind.

It seemed instinctive.

He had no tribe, no mate.

That was not a problem as a human: it was intolerable as a hominid.

Why the top of the mountain would yield anything of that nature, he did not ponder.

His experience was his guide: the plains below, he remembered, had not provided any sustenance in that regard.

So, the path above was the only way.

His senses were fully come alive.

He sniffed the air keenly, and listened intently to every sound the wind, and falling tree limbs, made.

He now sought, and found, easier paths up the hill, by trying out various footholds with intense care and concentration.

He did not lose his footing anymore, but was sure-footed, and agile, like a mountain goat.

He used tree limbs to test for weak holds, often using them as supports.

As a hominid, he seemed far more dextrous than as a human.

CHAPTER FIFTY-SEVEN
Perspectives

The Empire of Man had not lasted that long.

Mere dinosaurs had ruled far longer.

Species came and went with monotonic regularity.

So the Debacle of Man was not specially poignant, except from a human vantage point.

That point of view was *anthropocentrism*, the idea that the universe exists but for the succor and solace of Man.

Various religions, Christianity, Islam, *etc.,* subscribed to that view.

Seeing the universe as an Anthropic universe.

It couldn't be that in a realist sense - since it appears, from the point of view of sheer economy, too big a universe for the consumption of mere humans alone.

But it could be that in an epistemic sense.

After all, if there is no one left to behold it, what happens to the universe?

We don't know.

We cannot know.

But we can, naturally, speculate.

He was the Last Descendant of the Empire of apocryphal Adam.

Perhaps, he would stumble upon the truth of the universe.

By accident.

CHAPTER FIFTY-EIGHT
Greed and Power

How could it have come to pass?

How could they that built the Pyramids, and laid cables from end to end of the poles, allow such a finite limit to human possibilities?

Actually, the question itself contained the answer.

The pyramids were built for/by Power, the cables for/by Greed.

The Two Eternally Endemic Drives of Man.

Building bombs, and detonating them, was part of that very same *logos*.

So, the lot of 'homo sapiens' was predetermined.

Men 'improved' upon hominids in the vital regard also of the technologies of Violence.

"Ignorant armies, clashing by night" were akin to rams battling it out , head to head, on some forsaken mountain crag.

Men were born to destroy themselves.

The irony of evolution is quite remarkable.

It vests men with Violence.

And women with Pacifism.

Hoping, perhaps, for 'balance'?

But nature, if it intended it thus, had goofed.

The consequence was not a permanent *War of Genders,* but Final Annihilation - of both.

And Others.

Our Hero was in no need for such reflections upon karma.

He was now just the sensate animal nature quite intended him to be.

Left alone - neither at Peace, nor at War.

Simply trying his organic best to acclimatize.

And survive.

CHAPTER FIFTY-NINE
The She

The vapors showed no sign of abatement.

The thick darkness, no sign of thinning.

And the mountain, no sign of permitting easy reach to its apex.

Indeed, the apex was still invisible- though he had climbed tenaciously, for days.

The mountain did not give in.

He did not give up.

Both were born of nature, imbued with their own distinct logics of existence.

Dreams, and recollections, often impeded his natural progress up the perilous slopes.

One such was specially disarming.

He recalled his first meeting with his wife, owing to no particular stimulus.

It seemed alien now, as an image.

He had gone for a long walk in the woods.

And there he saw her sitting on a tree stump by a pond, motionless.

He too had stood unmoving for a long time.

She appeared absorbed in her thoughts, but with her eyes fixed on the pond.

Soon, mesmerized by the stillness, he too sat down, unmoving.

The tall trees formed an arcadian canopy high above them.

Shafts of light, penetrating the grove, glanced upon the mirrored surface of the lake, shimmering like golden spears.

Hours later, she had turned to him, not noticing him, slowly.

Still waters, she whispered, can run so very deep.

He had listened, but said nothing.

He had remained there, long after she had left.

And returned many times over, sometimes to find her there, similarly situated.

Why she had chosen that one grove, of a dozen others, he could not say.

It seemed right.

Still, silent, and spectral.

Once, she had come in with her horse which fed quietly by the trees.

Sometimes, he would come in with his dog which, though naturally rambunctious, would , quite remarkably, in that grove, curl up on a rock - and muse.

They had rarely spoken.

One such afternoon, they were both standing by the edge of the pond.

Suddenly, a quite amazing shower of light illumined the bower.

As if the trees had parted, to let in a full glaze of light that poured down like a cascade of iridescent glitter.

It was so dazzling that it was impossible to be restrained.

She had turned and smiled, the light burning on her face, catching her curls in a blaze of fire.

That instant he knew what he had wished to say.

It was, in retrospect, a magic grove.

After she had left at their final parting, he had returned to the grove.

Hoping to Recreate that time.

But it was not to be.

The pond was still.

The trees silent.

And the light , almost grey.

He knew that nothing again would bring back that blazoned hour.

CHAPTER SIXTY
Vanity

The giant Pyramids still stand.

Spectacular, and magisterial.

But why?

To what end?

Who left of the band that built it, died in it, died for it?

Like man's incorrigible vanity, they still stand tall, a Testament to Vacuity.

Immune, apparently, even to nature's ravages.

Men know how to build.

But they also know, even better, how to destroy.

Indeed, little they build that they do not destroy.

One time, or other.

New civilizations are built upon the Ashes of the old.

Vanity upon Vanity.

CHAPTER SIXTY-ONE
Universe

Even without the influence of dreams, his now savage heart would fill at times with ineffable yearning.

All things turn to the sun.

The very planets revolve around it, in a cosmic love dance, taking years to consummate.

Pulled inward, we die like moths in a fire.

He looked upwards, and could not see the sun.

Therein the likely meaning of looking to the heavens, in piety.

The heavens are where the Sun is, the Center of our Little Universe.

It gives us all life.

It is our visible god.

But it is also a burning, searing, god.

One that will, in turn, like false gods, also die.

Returning us to the darkness we all hail from.

His rationale for climbing could not have been pre-given.

He was seeking his own source of life and light.

It is where we are pulled in by our own materiality, the molecules that animate us.

Even humans cannot escape the Gravitational Lure.

We are all One with the Universe.

We are the Universe.

He was seeking now but to return to it.

CHAPTER SIXTY-TWO
The Way

Where did we lose our way?

When did the felicity of hearth and home give way to the reign of profit and power?

When Men triumphed over Women.

When Masculinity overcame Femininity.

When simple emotions were put paid by the Vampire of Reason.

It is what we know – love or hate it as we might - today as *Modernism*.

Man is not a reasoning animal.

But a huddling one: a mammal , a heat-seeking animal.

Home is where that 'heat' is.

But man stepped out of his lair, misled by Egoism.

And could not find a way back home.

Instead, he tried multiple dodges, escapes, and Exits.

But they were not to tame that original, artificial, Estrangement.

Or overcome the Primal Yearning.

For Home.

CHAPTER SIXTY-THREE
Intuition

He, too, was seeking his home now.

And could not rest until he found it.

It was all instinctual.

He had gathered brambles he could eat, and found a way to hoard them.

He had sat all day polishing a stone until, despite the darkness, he could see his own visage.

It was barely visible, but enough to have him turn away.

Covered by hair, as thick as the brambles around him, he looked now like an ape.

Like the creature he really was.

An erect ape - one who walked upon hind legs only upon occasion.

But still an ape.

One day, he had produced a spark, a thin point of light, by rubbing stones together.

Another day, he had weaved reeds into a sort of a cloak, less rough and thorny than his earlier garb.

Similar ingenuity had produced a form of sock-like footgear that protected his feet from the friction of the rocks.

From devolution to evolution was quite a rapid process.

The climbing had become much less arduous.

CHAPTER SIXTY-FOUR
Evolution

How did life evolve?

A single cell had to be able to split, reproduce.

Could chemical reactants generate life, *sui generis*?

Or did it take a Maker to breathe life into the First Organism.?

In a Magical universe: either, even both, was possible.

Maya had room for both.

The issue of the First Chicken, the first whale, may not be resolved by the linear Logics of biology.

It takes an extra leap – of Belief.

Magic is quite sufficient; recourse to 'god' may well be overdoing it.

The universe may be a Collective Delusion – of sentient Beings.

And when the Last Being is gone?

What then?

CHAPTER SIXTY-FIVE
The Game

As far as he knew, he was the last being.

The Great Game of the universe was almost played out - but for him.

What would the Master of Revels inspire now?

What new trick had 'god' up its sleeve?

Our hero, now a dual self, did not know, or care.

Instinct had suppressed the wrong kinds of questioning.

Instead, it was teaching him the simple skills of Adaptation.

And he was starting to excel in it.

One day, unaccountably, he ceased his incessant labors of climbing.

After dining on a treat of nettles roasted in fire, he lay down and hummed a nameless tune.

It was like a song.

The weariness that had dogged him had lightened.

He smiled, as he hummed the rough, toneless, melody.

He had rediscovered pleasurability.

Turning on his side, he carved pictures, in the dirt, with a long stem.

Peering at them in the dark, he saw what he had drawn. It was an entire spectacle.

Of her, the boy, and the dog, in outline.

He sat up from his supine position.

The picture was highly disturbing.

His sub-conscious was still vested with memory.

He erased the mural with his feet.

Standing up, he howled a long mournful howl, much like a wolf, or a coyote.

The sound reverberated against the mountainside, returning in loud echoes.

CHAPTER SIXTY-SIX
Species Death

There is a cosmic memory written in our cells.

It is accessible, provided the mind does not invent escapes and excisions.

It requires no special Act of Retrieval.

The memory is not only of the Past.

Or, the Present.

But of the Future as well.

The universe is aware of both its own creation, and its coming Extinction.

Every last sub-atomic particle of it.

Consciousness is energy, energy is consciousness.

And it pervades All Things.

Animals live in the Twilight of that Knowing.

Humans have evolved to the point of glib concealment of that information.

To their eternal Detriment.

Our hero was strictly speaking neither human nor animal, but in that hominid state that is the very essence of our species-being.

Led by instinct, and unconscious reason, he could easily surmount his environment, but there was a new, hitherto unknowable, cosmic singularity.

He was aware, now, of the Death of the Species.

And even instinct was powerless in the face of that terrible Intuition.

The Last Dinosaur may or may not have experienced a similar emotion.

CHAPTER SIXTY-SEVEN
Devolution

He was still surrounded by the thick gloom of vapors, despite the days of climbing.

What if the noxious vapors had buried the mountain top?

Then, he could never see beyond.

But that thought was not on his mind anymore, since he was not 'thinking' anymore.

Instinct pushed him to climb now, in the direction of where sunlight, fresh air, and even companionship, may lie.

The absence of conscious reason was no disability, apparently, since instinct was a near-perfect substitute.

The thinking mind is also a fearing mind.

The uses of the mind might have become clear to him now, had he been able to think.

It is there to protect, serve, defend.

Instilling Caution, by garnering a roster of negative experience as safeguard and screen.

Which may be why so few deep thinkers are persons of Action.

But action was all he was about.

Like an arrow, he climbed, all his energies focused as one.

The universe was not unkind to hominids.

It let them act without fear of consequences.

Fear was a learnt behavior.

A very poorly learnt behavior.

It is the sure sign that the hominid has devolved - into a human.

CHAPTER SIXTY-EIGHT
The Law

The *Anthropic Principle* has it that the universe is designed for us humans.

That would make earth the center of the universe.

As a purely natural proposition, the notion merits little attention.

But it is true, more trivially: the world is our center, if not the center of anything else.

Cosmology can cut either way, though.

One can believe that the Incalculable universe is an expression of the power of an Immeasurable god.

Or, that our very inconsequential scale and size, in relation to nature, is an indication that , even in the natural scheme of things, let alone the supernatural - we are quite trivial.

It is a real property of the universe to foster Contrary hypotheses.

Its truth is supported by the existence of conflicting paradigms , that are inconsistent with each other.

So Plurality is the natural, lived, experience.

It is a sort of a Law of the Universe.

Oneness is Delusion.

And yet, there is no Duality.

It is neither dual, nor Non-dual.

It just is, what it is.

The universe is, thereby, Paradox and Delusion.

Maya.

It's a Magical universe:permitting, and prohibiting , all things.

CHAPTER SIXTY-NINE
Singularity

Our hero was the last living mammal, possibly, albeit in a still living planet.

How are we to establish his existence, his *Singularity*?

To do so would be to exist independently of him as a sentient being.

But that was impossible.

So, his existence could only be verified existentially.

Descartes would be right - but only in his case.

He thinks, therefore he is.

There can be no independent confirmation.

The story of the Last Human cannot be biography, only autobiography.

But one that cannot be read by others.

This would be true also for the very First human being who had to invent/discover, as he/she went along, watched only by uncomprehending hominids.

Was there a first human?

Can there be a last?

In a dream, all is possible.

CHAPTER SEVENTY
Life, and Death

As he climbed, an odd yearning took possession.

Much of him did not wish to follow him in his strenuous climb.

Indeed, a significant part of him wished to stop - even jump off the heights into the abyss below.

He remained dimly conscious of this, the prepossession oft-times slowing his climb.

The Life Force beckoned up.

The Death Wish wanted him down.

Evolution had this logic to it.

He had become nature's Mistake.

By himself, he could not propagate.

His existence was a unilateral tax/drain upon nature, which seems to believe in give and take.

The fabled, if apocryphal, instinct of the lemming, could only be a species-property, but he was experiencing it as a Society of One.

What could happen?

Which Force would triumph?

Every now and then he stopped, unaware of the Great philosophical/biological Struggle battling within him.

But the very stoppage was a reflex of the struggle.

His very Organon was in revolt.

CHAPTER SEVENTY-ONE
The Precipice

The anthropic *Geist* is unto itself.

Species are Mini-universes built upon the same properties of nature, in general.

But there is synergy, and symbiosis, to this geist.

It feeds upon its environs.

A universe without humans is not merely conceivable, it is an apparent fact of evolution.

But it is only conceivable, *After the Fact.*

For only humans would care to speculate on the nature of the universe, without humans.

However, a universe without humans, after the arrival of the hominid species, is a more difficult matter.

With humans gone, nature loses its anthropic meaning — meaning, it ceases to exist in a Meaningful way.

Our hero bordered this crevice, this *Epistemic Precipice.*

He was at the Margin of Meaning, of evolution, of anthropic existence.

Nature had now stilled his humanness - *via* instinctual triggers - so as to absorb him effortlessly into the biosphere.

He was fused with his dark world.

All that was left was the Final act/event of extinction.

CHAPTER SEVENTY-TWO
Murals

He plodded on, driven by determination.

The clouds did not lift, nor lighten.

The vapors still made his eyes blanch.

Foot by weary foot, he climbed onwards- and upwards

Nothing could really daunt him.

He moved like a tiger in the jungle, responding only to the stimuli around him.

The mind had made its quietus, and obstructed him no more.

Time was of no consequence, even were he to care to measure it.

The Circadian rhythms would have to work latently, unconsciously.

There was neither inspiration, nor imagination.

Just a dogged Will, charged by instinct alone.

The Abyss below was as invisible as the peaks above.

To jump, or to climb, had become a matter of indifference.

The choice between living or dying was being made, every minute, after a fashion, but with no real clues as to process.

A mountain stays put, out of inertia.

He was living on the same basis.

Every so often, the clouds would burst, showering him.

In one such downpour, he ducked into a crevice that turned out to be a cave of sorts.

He huddled inside, waiting for cessation of the storm.

Huddled in a fetal position, he fell asleep.

When he awoke, the mini storm had subsided.

With much effort, he managed to start a fire.

While warming the cave, it also cast eerie shadows on the cave walls.

His eyes followed the shadows, like darts, as he sat warming his limbs.

His glance was then arrested by what the dancing light revealed , in swiftly fading/reappearing images.

He stood up, and took a pace forward to the wall of the cave.

As the fire crackled behind him, its light now revealed the full aspect of the cave wall.

The wall was painted over with figures.

Human and animal images, engaged in various actions.

He rubbed the dust off the etchings, to get a clearer look.

The pictures did not register with him, though he stared long and hard at them.

He returned to his perch by the fire, though with an eye that still casually played upon the figurines on the wall.

The fire engaged his attention, but its whirling flames, and the shadows they cast, kept distracting him - causing him to glance again and again at the etchings.

The glassy look in his eyes was replaced by a low flame that kindled every now and then.

His anthropic memory had been piqued by the pictures of humans, in struggle with fellow hominids.

He did not sleep, but kept vigil by the fire for a long, long time, staring at the wall.

He rose, and touched the figures with his fingertips, running his fingers slowly all the way around their contours.

He was rapt in attention, unblinking, as he repeated the gesture over and over.

After a small eternity, he slipped down the side of the wall to his knees, crouching thus, hugging his knees with his arms.

Outside, the wind howled, and the vapors reeked as usual.

But he was unaware.

He was Crossing Over.

CHAPTER SEVENTY-THREE
Remembrance

Remembrance is an anthropic necessity, but one laden with pain.

Planetary life-forms all pass away, sooner or later.

And memory can only be the graphic one of loss, dispossession, decay, and death.

Mammals, elephants especially, seem to understand death, in however incomplete a way.

Our protagonist had been in a species of a mercifully deep sleep.

He was possibly about to awake.

Nature had lulled him, but dire anthropic memory was returning him to his genotype.

The human differs from others in its capacity to comprehend pain - for which there is no cure.

CHAPTER SEVENTY-FOUR
Original Sin

He was a Cosmic Hypothesis now, existing only within his own parameters of consciousness.

The collective consciousness of which he was part had vanished, leaving him quite marooned.

Only memory, and even more, pain, could connect him now with all that was no more.

He could, as the last hominid, carve his own Laws of Devolution within the grid of cosmic space-time.

Until now, this manner of Agency, set in nature, had claimed him, numbing his nature, and absorbing him into the delusive stardust of its own creation.

For unmeasured days now, he had been just a semi-conscious molecular life-form, guided by its limited preservational needs.

He had eaten, climbed, slept, danced, shouted, and jumped, all in a natural, mechanical way, spontaneously - much like horses relieve themselves whilst still feeding, unmindful of it all.

They were all expressions of his animality, of his bio-chemical drives.

Yet, inscribed within his psyche, was the memory of suffering - and that had now made all the difference.

Suffering, amongst humans, is not the intimation of mortality, nor even the loss of kith and kin, but the keen, razor-toothed intuition of the grand pointlessness of it all.

In that sense, all true suffering is caused by God.

The gratuitous Act of Creation is the most original, and banal, of all cosmic sins.

CHAPTER SEVENTY-FIVE
Perceptions

The sketches on the cave walls had jolted his natural state.

The men, women, animals, and children, portrayed there could not but break his trance.

But they didn't do so of a sudden, but gradually.

Slowly, his actions became less spontaneous and more controlled.

Slowly, his vision lost its blank fixity and was gathering focus.

The mind was awake, guiding him watchfully into the inner recesses of his psyche.

Until that signal moment when he, of a sudden, fell to his knees, sobbing.

He wept, on and off, for weeks, maybe more, all unmoving, whilst curled up in a foetal ball.

He had just come back from his strange sojourn in the Trans-Human warp of consciousness.

He had come back from the great Sea of Tranquillity that is our Non-Human nature.

Nature has attributes only in human perception.

Like god, which is its given name, it is without attribute.

CHAPTER SEVENTY-SIX
Metamorphosis

Metamorphosis is the State of the Universe.

But our hero had experienced more than his due share.

He set about his existence differently.

He could plot his own mini-evolution from anthropic human, to hominid, to a chastened human again.

He understood his ontological Dilemma.

It was unique.

In him, reality and delusion fused.

He was both the ontic, and the epistemic, simultaneously.

This gave him a degree of freedom unknown to humankind.

Choice of technique, of paradigm, of disposition.

He could, within limits, play god.

In the apparent absence of god, that would appear to be a credible alternate.

He reviewed his own recent past critically, and with care.

He was outside now of self pity and, also, of critique - of the universe.

It was, he felt, a game-playing universe.

He, like his past and present life, was part of a Great Game.

The rules were unknown, the strategies uncharted, the outcome(s) indeterminate.

What a challenge!

He proposed to rise to the occasion.

The game was a loaded one, one-sided in many respects.

But it didn't matter.

It was, he hoped, still a game of Chance.

The universe may hold all the aces, but he would still trump them, somehow.

Let the universe throw in free will, fate, and higher intervention - he would still be in the game because, being a lone isolate, Macro Laws simply did not apply.

His was an Indeterminate Quantum Universe of Micro freedom.

Somehow, sometime, the Makers of the Universe had decided to end it for all extant forms of life.

He, his family, his environs, had not mattered in their calculation.

Life-forms were but so much clay in the hands of the creators.

Life on earth, the living earth itself, was but a little experiment that was being called off.

He was the Terminus, the end of the line.

Or, so They/It had hoped.

But his mind was made up.

If there were a god, he would oppose it.

To his dying breath.

CHAPTER SEVENTY-SEVEN
Human Nature

He reviewed his own life, with much circumspection.

It was neither heroic, nor lowly.

He made the averages as far as error, blunder, and malintent went.

But, he had self-corrected.

And, thereafter, tried his best to be - a better man.

So, the punishment, if that's what it was, simply did not fit the crime - howsoever that might be construed.

Even in human ethics, that was not quite kosher.

And God had to be held to higher standards.

So that's the trump that Life held over the Universe.

It did not ask to be born.

And it was born free of sin.

So, it didn't, once conceived, need – let alone require- to be judged by an outside force.

Human existence is gratuitous - whilst Karmic Retribution, if true, is ill-conceived, cruel, and unusual.

True, men had destroyed each other, and their little world, all by themselves: but what force was it that let it all play through , unimpeded?

Who gave men their natures?

CHAPTER SEVENTY-EIGHT
Defiance

It was time for action, expression, and demonstration.

But, where could he start?

The time for grieving, even extended grieving, was over.

Now it was time for the *Sans-Cullotte* to rise up.

It was Defiance time.

But he would choose the way, the moment, and the means.

Strife of the kind he had experienced had to end.

No more climbing.

No more reaching for the heavens that weren't there.

No more struggle to escape.

It was time to rest.

He had earned it.

Stretching his limbs lazily he lay down, curled up, and fell into a deep slumber.

BOOK TWO:

THE RETURN

CHAPTER SEVENTY-NINE
The Waking

When he awoke, the terrain ,at first , seemed unfamiliar.

The Miasma had lifted.

The Mountain had vanished.

The air was clear, and the landscape looked far more hospitable.

He navigated just a little, and started to feel/sense vague signs of remembrance.

The crop of rolling hills looked familiar.

The woods that flanked them were those he thought he knew.

Indeed, he wasn't far from home.

No particular emotion surged within his heart.

He walked on now, on a well-trodden country lane leading, he knew, eventually, to his home.

The fields, on either side, looked seeded and kempt.

He didn't care to run his eye over them.

He passed by an object in the ditch by the lane that he thought he recognised.

The twisted remains of his son's first tricycle.

He barely gave it a second glance.

The wicket gate that guarded his yard was swinging on its hinges, moved by a heady wind.

Walking through it, he entered his home.

It was early evening, and the front porch was bathed in the rosy pink of the setting sun.

On the laundry line, that was strung to one side, there were clothes ruffling, and fluttering, in the wind.

He walked in through the open front door.

The house was empty, yet looked clean and swept.

He went into the kitchen.

The gas stove was on: indeed, something was cooking in the oven.

The radio was blaring country music.

He opened the refrigerator door: it was fully stocked.

He walked back to the bedroom.

The bed was made: and flowers that would have been fresh but the day before, lay in a bowl by the sideboard.

He went to his son's room.

All his toys were neatly arranged on the shelves.

Walking out, he stopped, turned, and looked again at a photograph that caught his eye.

It was a photograph of their son, taken when he was barely three, or so, years old.

He walked over to his study: his papers and books were all neatly stacked on his oak desk.

He sat down in the chair, mechanically.

The Game, he knew, was on.

CHAPTER EIGHTY
Home

He had fallen asleep, but woke to the sounds of crashing car gears outside, followed by the whoops of a child, and the barks of an excited dog.

Moving to the window, he saw his wife, their son, and the dog, getting out of their old truck.

His wife was carrying an outsize grocery bag.

Their son was sucking on a lollipop.

He sat unmoving, and heard the front door open and close noisily.

His dog came scampering up, and pawed at him.

His wife greeted him, from the passageway, and went on into the kitchen.

Their son was still in the front yard.

He stood up, and looked out the window.

There he was, bouncing a ball against the barn wall.

He couldn't have been very much more than five years of age.

He had re-entered his world, but at a time *previous* to having left it.

CHAPTER EIGHTY-ONE
Existing

At dinner, he said nothing.

His wife talked about her PTA meetings.

His son sat on a high chair, and tossed bits of food at the dog.

You seem preoccupied, said his wife, something the matter?

He looked at her.

No, nothing's the matter.

We need to sell the truck, she said, it's making weird noises. I think I'd like…

A red Chevy pickup?, he asked.

Why, yes – how did you know?

He shrugged, without comment.

After dinner, he excused himself.

Need to go for a little walk, he said.

His wife looked at him.

Sure nothing's the matter?, she asked.

He merely smiled, and walked out.

Reaching the clearing in the woods, where he had first laid eyes on his wife, he sat down by the rocks.

Bending down, he looked into the still, clear face of the pool and saw his own face.

He fancied he looked younger.

Judging by their son's aspect, a good many years younger.

It was a magic wood, and he looked around.

Am I to believe I exist?, he asked.

The pool rippled.
The tree leaves rustled.
Yeah, right, he sighed.

CHAPTER EIGHTY-TWO
The Milky Way

He lay in bed that night, unable to sleep.

His wife was asleep beside him.

He touched her hair, gently.

She did not stir, but continued to breathe, rhythmically.

He stepped off the bed, on tiptoe, and walked over to their son's room.

The little boy was asleep, clutching his teddy.

He stole out of the house quietly, and stood in the front porch looking up at the heavens.

The stars were all decked out, and then some.

No vapors, nor mists, to block them out.

As yet.

He stared intently at the great swirl of the Milky Way.

"You don't really care about any of us... do you?", he whispered, but answer there came none.

He fancied he saw a shooting star, like a sneer, streak across the hills.

He sighed, and walked back to the bedroom.

CHAPTER EIGHTY-THREE

First Moves

To know the past is to be wise.

To know the present is to be prudent.

To know the future is to be benumbed.

To know all three dimensions is to be a god.

He had now been given the opportunity to be God.

That, surely, was the First Move in the Great Game.

How would he play it?

Was he to simply relive his days?

But, already, with such manner of thoughts, he was living differently.

Could he alter his known past, by actively conspiring against it?

Better still, could he, perchance, save the world now, for having seen the future?

He couldn't sleep that night.

Knowledge, like freedom, imposes a burden of choice that ignorance doesn't have to worry about.

At breakfast, his wife asked whether he was to accompany her to the town meeting the next day.

To her surprise, he assented.

Too readily for her not to notice.

She smiled wryly.

How did you know I wanted a red Chevy?, she asked.

Same way I know you'll be nominated City Councilor, he said.

City Councilor... but I am not running for office, she said.

Just wait and see, he said.

CHAPTER EIGHTY-FOUR

Explications

He knew what was coming.

Clearer than anyone else.

What should he do?

Should he bare all?

Who would listen?

Who would believe?

Perhaps, he could start with her.

After she made Councilor - she was nominated, and elected, the very next day - he sat her down.

I have much to tell you, he said.

And he related it all, not sparing any detail.

She stared at him.

So, that's why you've been acting strange.

He looked at her.

Do you believe me?, he asked.

Well… there is the red Chevy thing… and my being elected and all…

So, do you?

She stared at him.

Do you seriously want me to accept the fact that, in the very near future, we are all, excepting you, going to die?

I didn't say anything about accepting it: do you believe I am telling you the truth?

Well…

So, you don't really buy it?

It's not quite that – it's that I don't know what to believe: it's something to do with the way you are - you see everything so very differently than others. You talk to the trees.... .you believe in astrology... you think the world's an illusion.

What if I predicted everything to follow for the next few months: what then?

Ok; that might be persuasive, but I would still like to know how you were there then, and are back here now. It's all too much to swallow.

Is it?

Don't you see it? Can't you see it from my perspective? It doesn't make any sense.

Would you like to believe it?

No, I don't really think so. Because if I did, there would be such a profound loss of meaning. The real world would be inexplicable.

It is inexplicable.

Only in some profound sense: at the mundane level, it's all pretty straightforward. No mystery to anything, really.

And what would make you believe?

I don't think anything could - it defies Reason. Experience. One can't live without those two Axials.

My god.

What?

Nothing: something that just occurred to me whilst listening to you.

What is it?

Oh, it wouldn't matter.

But tell me.

He smiled, and gave her a hug.

Another time, he said.

CHAPTER EIGHTY-FIVE
Prophets

Prophets turn up on earth routinely, and divine things both Good and Bad.

They perform miracles, defy natural laws.

It gets them attention.

Maybe, even a following.

But it really doesn't last long, in essence, though their ideas/ideals are preserved, if in mummified fashion, by the faithful, and the faithless, for aeons.

Fundamentally the (male) Anthropic being is not a Great Seeker of solutions to life's mysteries, but a sensate creature who lives by, and for, its passions.

It is led by hunger, greed, ambition, and other such simple animations.

That's its Anthropic nature.

So much is but native to its design.

So, the Prophets come and go: and leave the world virtually untouched, unscathed, despite their Miracles and their Psalms.

Here he was with the greatest story ever told - but his own wife wasn't ready for it.

Siddhartha might have pleaded with her in vain.

Or, Mahavira.

So, why do *They* come?

If they were divinely inspired, they sure got their inspiration skewed.

Of course, some fared better than others.

Some got themselves plain martyred.

Why would anyone follow any one who got himself/herself crucified?

That's what ordinary people often did to prophets

Prophet, beware.

CHAPTER EIGHTY-SIX
Politics

He went with her to the town meeting, and observed the unimpressive passion play of Electoral Politics.

Politics routinizes everything.

Even World Crises.

They formed Committees to Save the World, one meeting at a time.

He wished to tell them they were nuts

That they would all, soon, cease to be.

That they should all hug each other, and pray that the Inevitable didn't happen.

Maybe, form a Human Chain.

Maybe, all together, let out one long Primal Scream.

But, that didn't happen.

Instead, they passed resolutions, declaimed boldly, and clapped in wild enthusiasm – as though success was theirs already.

You'd think the little town hall was the United Nations, or the US Senate, the way they carried themselves and their rhetoric.

His wife's eyes were charged with a singular light.

She looked beautiful, with her determined chin and her resolute words.

He merely stared at her in wonder.

And felt guilty.

Perhaps he should have stayed home with his little boy, but he had promised her.

Time was so short.

CHAPTER EIGHTY-SEVEN
The Future

To know the future.

How appealing the notion is!

What would most of us give to acquire that kind of foreknowledge?

But, what if we did have it?

Would it alter anything?

Would we be happier?

Calmer?

No.

The Anthropic Crisis lies in the Finality of Death.

Of sudden, even unexpected, death.

Foreknowledge of death is no great blessing.

It makes the inevitable that much more inexorable.

It takes away Hope, which is sop to so many of us.

He pondered his lot.

It was not a pretty one.

Everyone would die, in the immediate future, save him.

What could be done about it?

How could it be done?

Was god letting him rewrite the Script of evolution?

If so, why?

To let it go as scripted?

Or, to Interrupt it?

What are you thinking of?, asked his wife.

Not sure, he said.

Tell me.

O, about everything – and, nothing.

She didn't sleep well that night.

In the middle of the night, she rose and went to the window.

There was a moon out that cast a pale gloom over the farmyard.

He stirred, and looked at her.

She smiled at him, wanly.

Maybe you did see it all, she said, just like you said.

He rose, and walked up.

She held him.

I am frightened, she said.

Only because it's night-time he said. In the morning, you will be yourself again.

She looked into his eyes, searching.

Could all be a dream?, he asked.

The red Chevy wasn't a dream, she said, have a look.

He stared out the window.

There was a new car in the far driveway.

He looked at her.

It's paid for by the Council, she said.

He stayed silent.

Ok, so you have seen it all, before, she said: except, I don't see how anything changes, in consequence.

CHAPTER EIGHTY-EIGHT
Entropy

He could hardly believe it all himself.

Would she really disappear down the driveway, forever, a second time?

Would he really read his last bedtime story to his little boy?

And then, what?

Would he be back in the Martian moonscape all over again?

It couldn't be.

There was no point to his being sent back in time, then.

It defied the Laws of Entropy.

Somehow, he was to effect Something.

For Others, surely.

It couldn't all be just a dead-end, set up just for him.

Nature was too niggardly to be that generous on account of but one hominid.

So, he had this task: of finding out what his 'mission' was, now that he was 'born again'.

He had to read the signs.

He had to divine.

And he had to do it soon.

Real soon.

CHAPTER EIGHTY-NINE
To Know

Knowledge is Power, in some instances.

Money, in others.

In still other cases, it's a source of joy or pain.

Or both.

We are not given complete knowledge, only partial.

He had seen much, known much: but he too, at the end of the day, was in the dark.

About Final Intentions.

The universe didn't share that, apparently, at any price, with anyone.

Nor Jesus, nor the Buddha.

It is the Anthropic Condition.

Wanting to, but not knowing.

It's another reason for the Perpetual Sorrow of humankind.

Endless grief, and eternal suffering – that, the lot of the enlightened hominid.

Not quite a model of Nirvana, leastways on earth.

He looked at his son, and suffered.

He looked at his wife, and suffered.

He looked at the beautiful universe, and suffered.

All things must pass.

It was inescapable.

It's simply folly to be wise – for then you feel the on-coming rupture with greater intensity.

He wondered whether ignorance was a functional gift, tossed in as an afterthought by an otherwise Uncaring creator.

The need to believe was powerful.

If we see order, we see god.

If we see miracles, we think them god.

If we read powerful Commandments, we think them emanating from god.

If our 'prayers' work, we believe it to be god's handiwork: if they don't, we see it not as an invalidation of godhead, but yet another affirmation of its inscrutable subtlety.

We make excuses for god, in a hundred tongues, every day.

Why?

Because, without blind belief, the prospect of death is even more baneful than it is.

For most of us, it is Ineffable Fear that turns us to god.

Perfect Fear moves us to temperance.

Perfect Love is said to cast out fear.

But perfect blindness will do it too.

Also, even better, perfect stupidity.

CHAPTER NINETY
Justice

He thought about it , intensely.

Is it a Just Universe?

Nature is red in tooth and claw.

The powerful eat the powerless.

Baby deer are ripped to shreds by lions.

Men kill each other with even less reason, and far more brutally.

The Earth, like much of the universe, is composed of great, big, burning streams of real hellfire.

Yet, we believe in an All-Compassionate god.

A kindly god.

A benevolent universe.

The daily evidence of our senses is enough to hang god.

But we don't.

We still hold It up as some perfect *Non-Pareil.*

Why?

God is everything, one might say, that we are not - or don't see, in this universe.

It is perfect, because the universe is imperfect.

But that is a measure , perhaps, only of our need for an opposite.

Indeed, and *au contraire*, the presumption that god is as bad or as good as the universe itself carries far more logical plausibility.

Supposing, as a research project, a Martian, were asked to

comment on the nature of the 'Maker', after observing human and animal history and behavior alone.

What would it write?

Not a tale of benevolence, surely.

Indeed, assume that god is pure Evil: and the world bears out the regal stamp of that hypothesis quite fully.

Just one minute's viewing of the evening news in New York City would confirm it; much as a single episode of a series on 'Animal Kingdom'

So, God is not born of our empirical experience.

It cometh from Someplace Else.

CHAPTER NINETY-ONE
Scenarios

He accompanied his wife to the meetings, when local.

When she went national, he stayed home with his son.

The world crisis was deepening.

With news to sell, the Media had already swamped the public with doomsday scenarios.

Half of Africa, much of Asia, and some of Latin America, was in deep economic crisis.

Starvation, famine, and rioting, were endemic.

Yet, the rich world had never had it so good.

Whilst Ethiopia starved, America was setting new, and improved, standards for obesity.

How heedless we are !

How thoughtless, how Unenlightened.

How determinedly Men march themselves to extinction.

Yet, to their credit, millions all over the globe, the Little People: women, workers, unionists, NGO's, were protesting, marching, and picketing - though to equally 'little' avail.

The leaders wrapped themselves in their respective flags, and fed their nations with the usual malarkey of having to destroy the world to save it.

He was impressed with his own wife: her energy, her enthusiasm, her courage.

We are that close, he heard her say, to a large women's audience, to Armageddon. Are you going to go on baking pies and vacuuming, or are you ready to get up do something about it?

You could have heard the knitting needles drop.

Do something, she said, to the startled women, don't leave things up to men: your husbands, sons, fathers, and brothers.

It's Your turn, Our turn now.

It's the New Millennium.

I have 3 children to watch over, said one woman, what could I do?

Get on the internet, said his wife, when the children sleep: hook on to the worldwide movement for peace and justice, make calls for them, hang out a sign of support by your gate. Get your husbands going, too.

Mine comes home and just flops, said another, then it's just tv and dinner.

Then wake him up, she answered, refuse to cook dinner. Turn the tv off.

There was a stunned, audible, reaction.

If he still doesn't get it: then go ahead, go on strike.

On strike?

Yeah, refuse him sex.

CHAPTER NINETY-TWO
Saying No

His son asked him what he might do, having heard his mother's talks.

Your homework?

There's no homework in first grade, dad: I meant what can I do to save the world?

He looked at his son. He looked so much like his mother.

So that's how we live on, he thought, in our children's visages.

I don't really know, he answered.

Dad, said his son, what are you doing about it?

Me?

Yeah, you.

I?... well, I support your mom, make sure the fields are tilled, the animals fed, that we have a roof.

No, dad, said his son, mom says we all need to do more, something extra.

Ok, so what do you suggest?

I'm going to work on a giant poster, for school.

Yeah?

It's going to say - Say No to War: Peace Now.

Sounds great.

And how about you, dad: what're you gonna do?

I?... I'll think about what I might do.

Promise?

Sure: I will. I… promise.

His son smiled. There she was again, in that smile.

He had no choice now: he had promised.

Out of the mouths of babes.

CHAPTER NINETY-THREE
Power

He had promised to think about it.

So he did.

A walk to the woods, where his quiet thinking spot lay.

The trees were tall, quiet, and majestic.

Under their aura, there was a certain primal, arboreal peace.

He could be still there, and think calmly.

What is the nature of the power we wield?

There was the power of the rich and the corrupt – the State - expressed in their mighty ICBMs.

Then the power of ordinary peoples, living, marching, struggling, and moving restlessly.

Yet, each seemed a mirror image of the other, despite their different motivations.

Why did neither seem right, though each was, apparently, inevitable.

Was there *Another* source of power?

He thought of Christ, and Gandhi, and Siddhartha.

Was that not power, too?

Did they not move millions at their bidding.

What manner of power was that?

Whence, its provenance?

How, why, was it different?

The trees looked down upon him.

The sun shone through the branches, scattering dappled shade and light.

The pool did not stir, but lay still, like it were empty.

If there were an answer, it was, maybe, right there.

In that Place.

In that Moment.

Of a sudden, he heard a twig snap.

Looking up, he saw a deer come to drink at the pool.

It had not seen him, amazingly.

It bent its graceful neck down, and drank.

Then it raised its head to look, and saw him.

Their eyes met.

Neither moved.

The almond eyes drank him in, as he stared back, motionless.

Slowly, it lowered it head again, and drank.

Then it darted its head back.

A little fawn came up from behind, to snuggle by her mother's legs.

The deer nudged it, and it, too, took a dainty sip of the waters.

The deer mother licked its head as it snuggled yet again.

He stood up, rising slowly.

The deer looked on, cautiously.

He moved toward them, noiselessly.

They continued to observe him.

He was now but a few feet away, when something, maybe a tree blossom, fell in the water, making a gentle splash.

The deer bucked, and then fled.

He watched them depart, sadly.

But, as he walked home, he felt he had learnt something.

About the apparent Meaning of Existence.

About Two eternal, ever-present conditions we live with.

Love, and Fear.

The State knew nothing of Love.

And the People, who knew Love, lived in awe of Fear.

He felt he knew now what he had to do, and, perhaps, all that he could do.

Maybe, he had not let his son down.

CHAPTER NINETY-FOUR
Crisis

Spectacular acts of violence, and sabotage, were rife in all corners of the globe.

There was precious little public safety, let alone political stability.

Revolution, civil war, and *Coup D'etats* , were daily occurrences.

A sense of doom, and impending chaos, were ubiquitous.

Of course the parties, the eating and drinking, went on as always - but more mechanically, without any real zest to them.

A day spent quietly at home was far more reassuring than the night out celebrating.

Distrust and despair were equally rampant.

A sense of hopelessness was descending on most.

Men in grey suits made patriotic Speeches.

Young(er) Men, in khakhi suits, made (equally patriotic) War.

Many others just huddled - and prayed for an end to the *anomie.*

He had spent the morning in reverie.

His wife was out on a daylong conference.

His son was at a neighbor's house, playing.

He had finished his morning chores around the farm.

The fields were ploughed, the animals fed and watered, the silos inspected.

He was sitting on the porch, listening to the manifold sounds of the universe.

The morning's wash swung lazily in the breeze, on the clothesline.

The dog was out somewhere - chasing birds, fruitlessly.

He was transfixed, remaining motionless for hours, though with eyes wide open.

Eventually his son came home , dropped off by a neighbor.

The boy greeted him, casually before rushing inside to the kitchen for his snack and soda treat, accomplished usually before mom came home to stop him from junking out.

The door he had slammed behind him swung to and fro , noisily.

Soon, the dog, hearing the sounds, came up to inquire, and disappeared indoors where he could hear it barking happily.

Time ticked on.

The sun dipped slowly earthwards, as dusk rose to envelop the sky.

A loud crashing of gears foretold the arrival of his wife.

He had been sitting still now for some 7 hours.

She pulled in, parked, and walked up to the porch.

Even the ritual peck on his cheek didn't seem to break his spell.

Busy day?, she inquired lightly.

He made no reply.

We passed a resolution, she said, It'll make the papers tomorrow.

He looked up at her.

There was elation in her face,

He remembered, in auguries of innocence, its younger visage.

She was still quite youthful, despite the furrowed brow.

The many-hued light of sunset played upon the porch.

This day is about to die, he whispered.

She stopped, on her way in.

Just look.

The sun, at that very moment, dived below the horizon.

CHAPTER NINETY-FIVE
A Collage

After dinner, he insisted on them all going for a drive.

It's important, he said.

They drove to the top of a small canyon ,where he stopped and got out the car.

The light, being a summer evening, was still quite sufficient.

Mother and son got out , and peered down the ruggedly steep ravine.

Wow, said the little boy.

It is beautiful, she said.

Yes: you both are, he said, softly.

She looked at him.

Sit down, he motioned.

They sat on wide, flat , slabs of sheer rock that lay strewn by the edge of the ravine.

He looked at them, and bent forward, taking their hands.

You are my World, he said.

I could not want more, nor have more , than I have right now, nor be more than I am right now.

She smiled, remembering the past.

But the real world is bigger than me, than you, than all of us.

In that universe, to that universe, we barely exist or are noticed.

He turned to his son.

We can't save that world, he said, it's a lot bigger than us: but we can save our world, this little world, that we each touch and feel with our hands.

What do you mean, dad?, asked his son.

I can't do giant posters like you: nor can I be a Town Councilor like mom, but I can do one thing: I can try and see that we always have each other, be with each other, raise each other, help each other so our little world, is just as it is now, forever.

Forever? she asked.

In our hearts, and in our spirits, forever.

And the world outside?

Is just a mirage, a dream, a collage.

What's a collage?, asked his son.

He smiled.

A great big cut-and paste picture, like your school poster.

But, for all that I can do, I still cannot save this world, our world, by myself - without your help.

I'll help, said his son.

He looked at his wife.

She grimaced, petting his hand.

It's getting late, she said gently, we should go.

He looked at her: she looked away.

CHAPTER NINETY-SIX
Love

That Love is the Answer has always been known, for aeons.

It required neither great insight, acumen, nor specialized knowledge.

Neither Jesus, nor Krishna, invented it as an Idea.

But the sensate life has many challenges, natural and social, that elide the simple resonance of that Answer.

Love is not always the perfect Antidote for greed, or ambition, caprice, or even sheer human need.

Regrettably, the Manifest Destiny of humankind is doom.

We face premature extinction not because of our inability to conceive of solutions, but of our routine unwillingness to sublimate our primary drives of instinct, principally of the masculine kind.

Love is the one philosophy that may not be preached, only practiced.

It is effective not in the preaching of it, but only in the practice of it.

So, he could not march up to the pulpits of this world and preach the gospel of love.

It had been done.

To mere words of that nature, the world remained but like the proverbial deaf adder.

He could, however, invest it, in his own Little Segment of this Anthropic universe.

In the hope he could, at least, create a small haven of

nurturance in the great ocean of competitive hatred that had enveloped the world.

What else could he do?

He had seen the future.

The world was not created to be saved.

It could not be saved.

If only people knew that, as he did - they might strive to save themselves, and their own personal loved ones.

That night, he paced the floor of the bedroom as the others slept.

Could he help any of It?

Could he make any difference?

Or, was everything flowing, like a swollen river, rushing headlong to an oceanic doom?

Dawn filtered in through the blinds, even as he still pondered, and still paced.

CHAPTER NINETY-SEVEN
Deeds

The next day's papers proclaimed the invasion of yet another Great Power by another.

The Deed was done.

The ramifications were yet unclear.

But the Peace, fragile as it was, was broken.

Stock markets shut down, armies placed on alert, and emergency laws proclaimed.

She rose from the breakfast table.

We will be in conference, she said, all day, maybe all night.

He looked at her.

There will be resolutions, declarations, and a delegate mission dispatched to D.C.

When will you be back?, he asked.

When it all gets done, she said, drily.

He watched her leave.

He turned to his son, after the boy had kissed his mother goodbye.

Wanna go horseback riding?, he asked.

Oh, yeah, said the little boy, love that.

All day they were out riding in the woods, picnicking by the woodside, late in the afternoon, as the horse grazed nearby.

Hey dad, said the boy.

Hmmm?

If you had a wish, a magic wish what would you ask for?

The moon, probably, he said.

No, serious, dad, insisted the boy.

He looked at the little face, and the horse that was now drinking at the pool.

For everything to be the way it is right now – forever.

Me too, said his son.

CHAPTER NINETY-EIGHT
Clouds

She didn't return for many days.

The news just got worse by the day.

Other nations had entered the fray, so it was getting to be a Global conflagration.

She came back late one night, emaciated and exhausted.

We achieved a lot, she said, We are now in active contact with a dozen nations and hundreds of NGO's. It's all quite exciting. The phones don't stop ringing. There is to be a national demonstration in D.C., next week. There will be representatives from across the world. I will be making a speech.

He pressed her hand.

Can you manage, while I am gone?, she asked.

He shrugged.

Don't we always?, he replied.

Good, she said, I don't want to worry about you two.

He smiled gently.

Whom do you wish to worry about?, he asked.

All of us: humanity, the world, she said, the nations at war, the people dying everywhere. So much has to be done, and so soon.

That is a lot to worry about, he said, rising.

We will stop the war, she said, and put an end to all the madness.

Don't forget to take your vitamins with you, he said.

What?

Your supplements. You left them behind last time. You need them.

How can you think of vitamins at a time like this?, she demanded.

I'm not thinking vitamins, my dear, he said lightly, I'm thinking of you.

CHAPTER NINETY-NINE
Rifts

One night, she didn't come home, but called to say she'd be held over.

She didn't return for a week.

The boy missed you, he said.

And I him, she said.

You should try and call when you can't be here.

I didn't have a minute.

He looked at her.

You had a minute he said, *sotto voce*, walking out.

She followed him out to the barn, where he cleaned up.

Do you think I don't miss him?, she said.

Do you, he asked?

She sighed.

So now you doubt me.

I'm sorry if it sounded like that.

She bit her lip.

I do what I do for all of us: for you, for me - for us.

I know.

Then why do you... take this attitude?

I don't know – maybe, I feel things differently.

Like what?

I don't know, he said.

Look, she said, all my life, all through this marriage, I stayed home, cooked and cleaned. I am not complaining, but it's a fact. Now I find that I am needed by others, thoughtful people, who seek my counsel. I find I am being taken seriously.

He looked at her.

No, that came out wrong: what I mean is I am doing something others, apparently, can't do as well. At a time when the world seems to have need of people like me who speak out. I am needed out there.

You are needed here, too.

I know: but you manage all right: you always did.

He kept quiet.

And I need to do the things I am doing. I have to do them. I must do them. I think them important. I know they are.

Ok, he said.

Ok?

Yeah, ok. Fine.

No: don't okay me aside. You come back from a fantastic journey, and tell me the world is ending. Do you expect me to go on baking pies after that?

I don't see the harm, he said.

I do, she said.

CHAPTER ONE HUNDRED
Cotton Candy

He sat on his tractor, plowing his little field.

The sun shone gently that autumn day.

His son rode with him.

Dad, said the boy.

Hmm?

Mom is on tv , and everything.

I know: isn't that great?

I wanna see her.

You will, she's back next Saturday, unless… .

I wanna see her before next Saturday.

He turned the tractor engine off.

Do you?

Yeah: I wanna see her in front of the tv cameras, makin' speeches, and all.

Really?

Yeah: can I, dad?

He looked at the boy. In his yellow straw hat and blue denims, he looked a picture.

Sure, he said, why not?

Really? You mean we can go?

Uh-huh.

They left shortly, and drove to town.

The streets were packed with people crowding into kiosks , catching up with the newest events on the world stage.

Signs, and placards, hung everywhere.

Nobody seemed to walk alone, anymore, but in huddles of two and three, chattering away.

The Town Hall was impossible to reach by car, so they parked in a far outdoor lot and walked up to the doors.

The mob outside, and police, made it impossible to get close up, let alone go through the doors.

He carried the boy on his shoulders, so he could see better.

Can't we go in?, asked the boy.

He looked about him, and had an idea.

I know, he said, let's take the back entrance.

Negotiating his way past the dumpsters, and parked cars, he found a back entrance, and slipped in.

Soon, they were in the overflowing hall.

Where's mom?, asked the boy.

He looked all over the stage. Then they saw her. She was speaking animatedly to a tall man, in a bow tie, gesturing the while, as a tv camera covered her.

There she is, said the boy, Hey, mom... .

His shout barely rose above the noise.

Father and son watched the interview from afar: after it was over, the tall man shook hands with her and embraced her.

She returned the embrace warmly, and then turned and walked away with him, touching the sleeve of his coat.

Mom, shouted the little boy.

She can't hear you, he said gently.

But I want her to, said the boy.

I have an idea, he said, how's about a great big dollop of ice cream?

The boy still strained to look after his mother, but she was gone.

Ice cream?

Yeah: cotton candy flavor, your favorite.

O boy, said the boy.

Let's go, he said, and carried the boy out.

They got home late, after having stopped at a pizza parlor, and taking in a movie.

The boy was asleep on the way home, and he carried him to his bed, shoes, jacket, and all.

CHAPTER ONE HUNDRED AND ONE
Goings-on

She came back Saturday.

He was busy sweeping up some bushes he had trimmed.

You didn't tell me you came to the Convention, she said the next morning, Junior tells me you both came and saw me speak.

How did it all go, he asked?

Well, we are going to the UN to speak, she said, as part of a national delegation.

Terrific .

Heads of State will be in the audience.

Wow.

The President is attending, too.

That is unbelievable.

Yes.

He looked at her. She was glowing, radiant.

Never seen you look this alive, he said.

Never been this alive, she said.

Must be the times.

Yes, it's the times.

He looked at her again.

I'm taking Junior camping, he said.

Camping?

Yeah, he wants to go.

Darn it, wish I could come.

I - yeah, we would both wish that, too.

But I can't.

I understand.

But I'll call you.

He nodded.

Have to leave to catch a plane.

Oh, shall I drive you to the airport?

I am getting a ride, she said; ah, there's my ride, now.

A gleaming town-car pulled up.

She pecked his cheek, and jumped in.

Tell Junior I'll miss him, she said.

The man inside, driving, waved at him.

He waved back.

It was the tall man on stage.

CHAPTER ONE HUNDRED AND TWO
The Gnome

That night, after his son had fallen asleep, he had a dream.

It was strikingly vivid and powerful, as if presented in Technicolor.

He was walking through a thick jungle and, clearing a specially difficult path through overarching vines, came upon a strange creature, in rags, perched upon the stump of a tree.

The image was so odd, and unexpected, that even within the dream he was finding it hard to accept it all as real.

The man had three eyes, one in the very center of his forehead.

He appeared to be either asleep, or in some deep trance, since all of the three eyes were closed.

As he edged past him, hoping to slip by undetected, the man opened one eye, his third eye.

Quo vadis?, asked the stranger, who looked like a garden gnome.

Huh, he said, startled, and not a little afraid.

Fear not, said the gnome, I am merely the voice of your own conscience.

You are what?

It's almost as if I don't exist… except in your own imagination.

What do you want from me?

Nothing, except clarity.

Clarity.

Clarity in all things.

Why?

Because, as your conscience, I wish always to be clear.

I am far from clear, he said, about anything.

I know: that's why I am sitting here in this wretched, steamy , jungle awaiting your awakening.

Awakening?

Yes: it is high time. Don't you think?

Is it?

I will ask you three questions, said the gnome. If you answer all three correctly, you will survive me - or else, you will never return to your native land.

I'm in my bed asleep, he said, so this is all a weird dream.

Maybe - but here is query number one: who are you?

I don't know.

Good. Now, where do you come from?

I don't know.

Right again, said the gnome, as if in glee. Now for the last query: where are you going?

I don't know, he said.

Terrific, said the gnome, opening all three eyes.

Now, you are ready, and open, for enlightenment.

The gnome rose slowly, still sitting, expanding like the hood of a giant cobra.

He seemed to have a million tentacles spreading all around him.

Come , my son, said the gnome, I will take you there myself.

No, he shouted, no, no.

His son was shaking him.

Dad, wake up, said the boy, you're yelling in your asleep.

He sat up, and hugged the boy.

It had all seemed all too real.

CHAPTER ONE HUNDRED AND THREE
Clues

He thought about the dream, the gnome, the three queries, and his own answers to them.

It was odd.

He had the same answer to all the three questions: yet the gnome seemed happy.

Why?

And what did any of that have to do with his enlightenment?

Was he missing something?

What was he missing?

He sat on the fallen trunk of a tree back of the farm house, pondering.

Hours went by.

He could hear his son playing with the dog, whooping and yelling.

He could hear the bees buzzing, and the drone of insects he could not have named , far away.

Again, there was that dream-like quality to it all, as in the prior night's dream.

Suddenly, there was a thunderclap.

A section of the barn collapsed right before his eyes.

He ran over to ensure that his son, or the dog, were not in there.

They were safe. Part of the barn was overloaded with produce , and had simply caved in.

He entered the barn, and started to pick up the spill of greens and vegetables, by hand.

Bending over, he picked up a head of broccoli, and was about to place it in one of the baskets when his head, suddenly, swam.

He tried to sit but failed, and fell to the ground.

He closed his eyes, but the world continued to spin, even though his mind was free and calm.

Enlightenment?

Three questions?

Oh, my gosh, he said, trying to sit up.

Could it really be that simple?

It couldn't. Surely not?

He started to laugh, and rolled over in stitches.

His son, and the dog, came rushing in.

You okay, dad?, said the boy.

Yeah, I am, he said, hugging them both. I am ok.

Gee, look at the mess, said the boy, looking to the ground covered with produce.

It's alright, he said, there's order in this chaos.

Huh?, said the boy.

O nothin', he said, just joshin' ya. Let's clean up.

CHAPTER ONE HUNDRED AND FOUR

Doom, with a View

That night, he sat on the porch.

The stars were on parade in the night sky.

So, that's all there was to it.

Human Vanity, in spite of it all.

There was death and danger, but that was just the nature of the amoral universe.

That much was simply innate and unchanging.

It was only humans that interjected valuations on the universe, good and bad.

Evil, of the motivated kind, sprang only from Vanity.

The Male Ego that cannot be still.

Not merely wanting more, but wanting to be more.

All our Anthropic tribulations spring from it.

Excise that one domain - and life is, until overcome by death, but routine existence, such as endured by all living things.

The sun rises, the sun sets.

People live, people die.

All as Un-extraordinary as breathing

Bring vanity in - and there are hills to climb, principles to prove, immortality to achieve.

Battles to fight, ideals to be ordained, and/or emulated.

We are stardust, but full of strange yearnings, stemming from that one, purely mortal, ill.

We know so little, expect so much.

How we hope to hang on to what we believe is ours on this planet!

Our Things, our Associations, our Family.

How nice to believe they are all ours, forever.

Nothing is forever, quite literally.

How cleverly religions exploit that human frailty, and promise us all a bountiful heaven.

Sign on the dotted line, turn over ten per cent, and you're all booked safe passage.

And then death becomes: a Doom with a View.

We don't follow realists, but those that offer to gaily, lavishly, nay recklessly, feed our delusions.

In that sense, ignorance is led by even greater ignorance.

North, south, east, west: the same yearning, the same exultation, the same pie in the sky.

But he had in the process of just that one dream become enlightened: the forest gnome wasn't wrong.

Those three questions were all the ones worth asking.

And, he had answered them all correctly, every last one.

What profound knowledge: what ineffable ignorance!

He had perfect knowledge - of his perfect ignorance.

He had said he didn't know.

In so saying, he had tackled the Riddle of the Universe.

There was no Key to it.

It was not 'meant' to be 'known'.

It just is what it is. And what it is, is but a cipher.

The great Buddha, one of the most profound thinkers of all time (Jesus was a lover, not a thinker: his ideas were such as assimilable by a 3 year old), had built his enlightenment on profound wisdom, gained in silence, over years of penance and abstention.

Yet he, but a simple organic farmer, was enlightened no less, in his equally profound ignorance.

In but one line, he could express his entire understanding of the universe.

We Know Nothing : but still, the Vanity!

The universe let itself be 'known', not understood, discretely, in tiny nano-bits, but the moment we got smug about it, it up and rewrote the script.

It is a Magical universe.

A Game-playing universe.

A universe reeking with Maya and Leela.

A universe of Probabilities only, defying the inane certitude(s) of men.

CHAPTER ONE HUNDRED AND FIVE
The Plan?

What could it mean?

He had been spared the Holocaust.

He had been allowed to return.

He had been permitted his meagre load of enlightenment.

Now what?

What was he to endure?

What was the Plan for him?

The universe had cared enough to let him be a survivor.

Why?

The Master, or Mistress, of Revels had something in mind, surely.

Well, he would divine it.

So, he had been sent back to discover: exactly what? That his wife had some minor, sundry interests other than he had known about?

No, surely not.

Then what? And , if but that, to what end?

Cui bono?

He sat up the entire night in much confusion, though he thought of it all as clear thinking about issues.

He had decided to take their little boy camping.

Sort of like fiddling whilst Rome was burning all around.

Why?

To prove what?

To run away from what?

He fancied an answer to it, in the early hours of the morning.

He was still in search of innocence, for him and his son, in a world that had destroyed that delusion forever.

And his wife?

She had to make her choices.

Philosophers, like theologians, might call it free will.

He didn't know what to call it.

CHAPTER ONE HUNDRED AND SIX
Exodus

World news had ceased to be of interest to the average populace.

Instead of watching the news, people were preparing for the worst.

The Exodus, away from cities and towns, prime targets in nuclear madness, had begun.

At first an uncertain trickle, it was a wanton flood now.

Trust in paper documents, and pledges, was already close to nil.

People were trading things and services.

Yet banks were open, and government offices flew the flag as if it were all still kosher.

The strait Image of Normalcy had to be maintained.

But it duped only the few.

Most people simply paid no attention, and went about safeguarding their lives.

The small percentage of the Unenlightened still clung to their delusions, but faith was eroding fast.

The cities were turning into urban no-fly zones.

But the country was still intact.

Whence the Great Migration to find the more enduring , even original, basis of social life.

The village, the family farm, the little community.

People were trying , stumbling, to find their way back to Eden.

CHAPTER ONE HUNDRED AND SEVEN
Escape

His son looked at him, as he was packing their backpacks.

Is mom not coming?, he asked.

He looked at the boy.

She might, he said.

Dissembling was better than lying.

She's not coming, said the boy.

He looked at the young face.

It was her face.

Maybe not.

Maybe not, and may be, amounted to the same thing: such are the vagaries of language.

I want her to come, said the boy softly.

Me, too, he said.

They got in their station-wagon, and headed out.

Where're we gonna go, dad?, asked the boy.

Deep in the Uintas, he answered, all the way into Yellowstone.

It would take them several days just to get there, it didn't matter.

It wasn't the getting there - it was the getting there.

The car felt empty.

There was a large, empty space in it.

Neither brought the subject up, again.

CHAPTER ONE HUNDRED AND EIGHT
Journey

The Journey to the Center of the Heart is a lonely one.

Neither spoke much.

The landscape around them opened up gorgeous vistas, but each was buried in clouds of preoccupation.

Even the eating and drinking, and overnighting by campsite fires, produced little real conversation.

His son sat roasting marshmallows, moodily.

Are we all going to die, dad?

He sat up.

What?

Like I hear in the news, everyone going to war and such...

He looked at his son.

It's not good, he said.

Why can't someone stop it?

Because... people... powerful people expect to gain by letting it go on.

That don't make sense.

I know that, but it still happens.

The boy looked into the fire.

Is mommy trying to stop the war?

Oh yes, he said, she sure is: trying harder than anyone else I know.

Yay for mom, said the boy.

Exactly.

Are you trying to stop the war, too, dad?

He stood up, and walked away.

Don't know how to, he said.

How about just like mommy?

'Cause I'm not mommy.

I wanna stop the war, said the boy.

Really - and how would you do that?

I'd go to Washington, and tell the President to just stop it.

And if he doesn't listen?

Then I'd tell Congress to fire him, and get us a new president.

He looked at him.

That's a terrific idea, he said, surprised.

The boy smiled.

Mom told me that, he said.

CHAPTER ONE HUNDRED AND NINE
Modernism

First, the uninspiring nature of what the universe has done to us living creatures.

Next, what we do to ourselves through stupidity, ignorance, and vanity.

And, to top it all, what adults do to children.

He stared at the boy, on the long ride home, surging with compassion.

He was only a little boy, and now he had to grapple with Big Things.

Sure, a dozen Psychologists would tell you it's all ok.

It's the Modern Condition.

I'm ok, you're ok, they're ok: no matter what.

He wished the poor boy could have been spared that.

Just for a few years longer.

But their fate was sealed.

He determined to keep him by his side.

If the Apocalypse did come, he would be holding his own gift of living life close to his bosom.

They arrived home, without event, though the traffic was abominable.

The boy rushed in to greet the dog that had been looked after by a neighbor.

He watched them both, boy and dog, as they frolicked.

The dog pushed his son to the ground, and was licking him as he rolled over in paroxysms of laughter.

He thought of his wife, and winced.

Where might she be?

Whom might she be with?

A rarity for him: helpless tears rolled off his cheek.

The sun was setting, and its dying rays enveloped the entire tableau in a glister glow of pale light.

Let there be night, he whispered.

CHAPTER ONE HUNDRED AND TEN
Tableaus

Save the world?

He sat up thinking, as the boy slept.

The world wasn't meant to be, couldn't be, saved.

All things must pass.

All destined but to perish.

What a delusion was the delusion of amelioration!.

Hope kills twice as effectively as hopelessness, and the dying lasts longer.

He would not hope.

The next day was Sunday, and he resolved to step into church, a first for him in decades.

The little parish church was not quite full for all the emigration to safer pastures.

The preacher was subdued.

The sermon asked for hope , in a hopeless world.

He looked past the pastor to the icon of Jesus laid sybaritically against the forlorn form of Mary.

The mother.

The dying child.

A Tableau of Human Life.

A hundred mothers have lived that scene, and a thousand sons have experienced it - backwards.

As the bombs fell, appearances of the Virgin were sighted everywhere.

In West Asia, sliced oranges had Allah inscribed in them.

In far India, tiny statuettes of the Hindu pantheon consumed vast quantities of milk, in front of rolling movie cameras.

Hoaxes, miracles?

Who knew?

And even fewer cared.

They were signs enough, though, that a world order was breaking down.

There may be little difference, from a perceiver's point of view, between a miracle and a mass delusion.

CHAPTER ONE HUNDRED AND ELEVEN
Signs

Signs, portents, everywhere.

Yet how many had really noticed?

How many of us notice anything, even normally?

We flit about our appointed ways, no time to lose or spare.

Yet, the universe had been laying out quite a spread of distress signals.

Impossible, one might think, not to have connected the dots.

Society had nearly imploded.

Politics had given way to war.

And the vast masses, rightly or wrongly, thought themselves powerless to affect outcomes.

We hominids are myth-making animals, and live staunchly by stories of ourselves - great ideologies, such as democracy, liberty, freedom, *etc.*

And whatever we believe is, in a certain sense, true.

What was he to believe?

He knew all would be destroyed.

What should he do?

By the time he figured an answer, there may be little left to figure: and, yes, he knew that, too.

For the time being, there was no specific impulse.

He continued to farm his piece of land, and spend every spare minute with his son.

He excavated, even exhumed, past relics of his childhood, and family history, so as to remember - when it was all gone.

The certainty of the imminent extinction seemed, oddly, not to weigh on him too heavily.

Mortality is a chronic burden of humans, so its sudden proximity could not be extra terrifying.

Besides, he was not programmed to deal with such knowledge.

As he tilled, and cropped, and threshed, and watered, one question continued to nag him.

What might he be doing to avert the impending disaster?

His own little boy had asked him that.

And he still couldn't answer it.

It kept him up nights.

CHAPTER ONE HUNDRED AND TWELVE
Tears

His wife kept up an itinerant family life, now here, now gone, now in-between.

She had already aged some.

The odd hours, the travel, the exhausting speech-making were all taking their toll.

One night, late, she called, in tears.

I want to come home, she said, sobbing.

Why don't you?, he asked gently.

I can't, she replied.

Why not?

Because they need me here.

Who does?

There was a pause.

They all do.

And how about little old us?, he said, softly.

I know, she said, that's why I'm crying.

Anything I can do?, he asked.

Are we all really gonna die?, she sobbed, it's so unfair.

I don't really know, he said uneasily, for sure.

I'll be back soon, she said.

When? he asked.

Soon, she said, real soon.

He paused.

Ok, he said.

CHAPTER ONE HUNDRED AND THIRTEEN
Exits

His neighbors, husband and wife, dropped in one day.

We're thinking of leaving, said the wife.

Where to?, he asked.

Not sure yet, said the husband,, someplace safe.

Is there *any* place like that?

Yes: we think we should move to Australia.

Australia?

Yeah. Nothing's ever happened there. Nothing's ever gonna happen there.

You think?

Sure.

So, what're you going to be doing there?

Well: we don't know. Maybe buy a small farm, land values are cheap down there.

When do you leave?

Not sure: we have to fix up a few things first, like sell our home.

Is anyone buying?

That's the problem: no, and we can't leave until we do. We need the money.

He could tell them that values would go on plummeting if the crisis continued, but he figured they must know as much.

And what are you guys going to do?, asked the wife.

Not sure, he said, you know my M—, is ever so busy , in D.C.

Oh, yeah, said the husband, they said, she's on tv a lot. Didn't know she had all that fire in her.

Me neither.

Course we can't support everything she says, you know, about our President n' things, said the wife sombrely, but she sure comes on strong. How's the boy?

Just fine, out playing in the field.

You shoulda had him a brother, she said, or a sister: ain't any fun growing up alone.

You're probably right, he said.

Darned shame, everythin' going to pot like this, said the husband.

Well, we shoulda done something sooner: the signs were all there.

It ain't our fault, it's the Chinese. They want war, just like the Ruskies, said the wife.

And us, what do we want?

Why, what's best for all, said the husband, surprised.

The President has gone to the UN twice this year, so   it's   not our fault, said the wife.

No sir, chimed her husband, it sure ain't.

He rose.

Well, I wish you both well, he said., with everything.

The husband looked at the wife.

Well, we came to ask you something, he said.

What?

You wouldn't wanna buy us out, would you?

No, he said, couldn't afford it - if I wanted to.

They rose.

Well, see you around, they said.

He watched them drive away.

CHAPTER ONE HUNDRED AND FOURTEEN
The Lover's Eyes

We only live once.

At least, in this life.

Time is the keeper of our dying flame.

To waste time is often contemplated and achieved, but is trivial: it is time that wastes us.

He had always lived as if each moment might be the last, as it could well be.

And yet there were those who squandered it, thinking it a free gift, ever replenished.

Today never comes back.

Yesterday is gone.

And tomorrow never comes at all.

He leaned on his tractor, and wiped his brow.

He had to think of something.

His son had climbed a cherry tree across the field, and was waving, whilst the dog barked, excitedly, below   .

Another picture-postcard, clearly.

And yet he looked upon it with fear, and regret.

His fear of evanescence was getting out of hand.

It was preventing active enjoyment of the ever-present present.

He turned off the tractor, and walked over to his son who waved cheerily at him.

He couldn't get enough of him, wishing he could have taken him down the tree and hug him fast to his heart.

But he shouldn't.

It would interrupt the idylls of a boy wrapt in the precious , unrepeatable, mesh of childhood.

He turned back, walked to the house, and strode on to his computer.

Finding a search engine, he typed in 'The Meaning of Life', and closed his eyes.

He opened his eyes.

Some cyberfreak had a picture of the mushroom cloud over Hiroshima, under the words.

He turned off the computer, and held his head.

Why?, he asked himself, closing his eyes.

Unbeknownst to him, he dozed off.

He awoke at the sound of the doorbell.

His wife was back.

He stared at her.

She blew him a kiss, and walked through the hallway,

calling their son's name.

Soon, he heard them engaged in conversation.

He peeked through the slit in the hinges of the door, and could see them hugging and kissing.

The picture was perfect.

The pageant is ready now, he thought, and quite complete - despite the dearth of himself.

Do I exist?, he asked himself.

No, came the answer: we dwell only, briefly, in Lover's Eyes.

CHAPTER ONE HUNDRED AND FIFTEEN
Family

The love of a child, for a parent, is transitory.

Nature does not cloud progeny with much sentiment in that area.

As we reproduce, we start to die faster.

The child is the full, perfect, replacement: and nature is simply biding her time.

Parents are gifted with perpetual nurturance, and their memory is painfully indelible.

How often do we think of our mothers and fathers, except in emergencies, when they are old and infirm, and living (and often dying) alone?

How often do we remember them, after they're gone?

Indeed, some of us wait for them to go anxiously, impatient at the slowness of the end.

Asymmetrical affections are the familial lot.

But it's not our doing, truly: instinct is the secret taped recording of god's commands.

Of course, we can rise above it/them: but above how many, and for how long?

So I am dead already, he thought.

He remembered the desperate sense of deprivation at their dolorous camping trip.

She was there, for not being there.

The Mother is the Center of the Human Family: she brings forth, succors, and sustains.

Her memory survives longer.

He buried his face in his hands.

Perhaps he had learnt something new that night.

CHAPTER ONE HUNDRED AND SIXTEEN
Woman

That night, she turned to him.

I am here to stay, she said.

Why?

I saw the light.

He looked closer. Her eyes were moist.

He thought of the tall man, but said nothing.

How may hearts does a woman have?, he wondered.

Many more than a man.

As nature's in-born Nurturer, and *Locus of all Human Hospitalities*, a woman must love many, in different ways.

With a pang, he realised that he was lowest on the scale of recipients of that sentimental largesse.

He heaved a sigh.

He knew now what he felt he had to do.

The pain of it might just kill him.

Nothing gold can stay.

He whispered:

I… I must leave you now.

What?

Don't ask why: but I must… I am impelled…

But why?

Because I love you both, and can't absorb the pain of it…

But…

I know: it must sound insane. All these years I was wishing you'd return, and everything could go back to normal, but…

But I am back, she said, look!

Are you?, he asked, meeting her eyes.

She looked away.

Or is it just… until next time?

She was quiet, crying.

We have never lied to each other, he said, so let's not start now.

What am I going to do?, she cried.

Live, he said, and raise our little one, there's enough money in the bank: take it all out. Don't leave it in there.

He will want you, she said.

Yes, he said, and I him: but I won't be gone forever. I couldn't.

She looked at him.

Remember, I know the future: I have seen it.

BOOK THREE:

THE EXILE

CHAPTER ONE HUNDRED AND SEVENTEEN
Succor

He rose early, before sun-up, and walked swiftly out the door.

The summer heat was still about the yard.

He had khakhi shorts on, a faded tea shirt, and worn hiking boots.

Avoiding the road, he made straight for the hills, through the fields, a mile or so away.

Before the sun rose, he was well on his way up through the low-lying ravines.

He carried neither food nor water with him.

This was to be his mock-serious, walkabout adventure with death.

He could suffer, perhaps, but he could not die, as yet.

That much had been foretold him.

Small woodland beasts scurried to get out of his way, as he pushed ahead , following along the dried up river beds that criss-crossed the ravines like sandy lattices.

Lazy carrion birds soared overhead, barely noticing him.

The hills had their own freshness, and he felt quite intoxicated with the musk-like scent of pine , maple, and spruce.

Bushes of wild roses, and daffodil patches, that crossed his path painted a warm portrait of summer gaiety that ill-fitted the turbulence of his confused heart and mind.

He saw little, and knew even less, of what lay ahead.

His concentration was only on the Oneness of his own Self through which all came, inevitably, mediated.

Hours went by, and he went deeper into the hills, and the thicker, darker, woods that approached as he gained in altitude.

Barely a few hours walking, and he had already left the signature of humans behind.

The sky rose up like a cobra's head ahead of him, with every step, and the blue firmament was all his eyes fixed on in their grand unseeingness.

The grass on the slopes, all round, was tinged with blue, an optical effect of some unknown kind.

The wind picked up , now and then, and brushed his hair high up so it stood erect like a waving bunting.

Succor me, he said, without moving his lips, to the universe: show me the Way.

CHAPTER ONE HUNDRED AND EIGHTEEN
Wanderings

Night fell all too soon: but he endured, and kept moving, guided now by lucent starlight.

How deceptively attractive the heavens looked!

He could have lain down right there, and looked upon the starry night forever.

But he was no casual wayfarer.

He was on a journey, led by That which he knew not , except he knew it existed - and moved him thus.

Ravine led to ravine, hill to hill: but his step was steadfast, and did not falter.

His rhythm was first organic, now mechanical.

Every pore in his body cried out to stop and rest, and great big swooning spells crashed upon his heavy eyelids, like tidal waves, inducing billows of sleep.

Maybe he would quite literally fall asleep, but that he could not help.

He would not lie down and seek it.

How long he walked that night, or how far, he couldn't tell ,but he woke up on a hillside just before dawn - having stumbled, and fallen like a log, dead to the world sometime earlier.

The shut-eye helped.

Energised once again, he sprang to his feet and scanned the horizon.

The sheer beauty of it quite enthralled him.

Yet in that very breathlessly ineffable beauty lay the cold, callous, impassive cruelty of an uncaring universe that cut like an icepick against the swell of his heart, gashing it with piercing pangs of rue.

He breathed a mute prayer into the heavens, giving thanks for the Inexpressible, then started out again.

The terrain changed, and became drier.

The ravines were steeper, and pockmarked, with caverns and water-crafted crevices.

The way forward was more arduous and involved real toil.

After much tax and trouble he had come to the crest of a high hill that overlooked a huge, dry valley that lay beneath.

He stopped for a drink at a nearby spring, by the side of which stood a great big tree.

It seemed to beckon him, and he slowly ambled up to the foot of its trunk.

The sun had risen high in the sky, and it was uncomfortably warm.

The shade of the tree, and the enervation caused by the lack of nutrients, were both powerful stimuli - cajoling him to stop there, and rest , until the sun shrank again in the west.

He felt the trunk carefully with his hands, and slid slowly down its length to slump at its spreading base.

The tree provided wonderful back support, and he thankfully leant against it.

Sundown saw him still lying , motionless, in a stupor, in that same squatting position, eyes closed.

CHAPTER ONE HUNDRED AND NINETEEN
Mirages

Thirty such sundowns came and went , and he still sat/lay there, bearded now, and thinner, but in that strange trance still.

He opened his eyes, several times, but saw nothing.

He had no cravings, felt no hunger nor thirst.

He felt nothing at all, and could scarcely move.

His breathing had become nearly still.

He was visited by hallucinations, dreams, mirages, and visions.

In some visions, he saw himself dead, lying against the tree, stiff as a corpse.

In another, he saw a big brown bear come all the way close up and sniff his motionless body.

In starker dreams, he saw fire and lightning and storms that buffeted him, leaving him perilously clinging to the tree as furious winds swirled about him.

In one dream, children, all dressed in white, walked past him in silent file, unmindful of his muted calls to them to stop and help.

Whirling dancers, and musicians, performed wild and indecorous operas that he could not comprehend, though they held him spellbound.

In one pageant, he saw his mother, his wife, and his son, walk past him , reverently strewing flowers over him, as if he were dead.

He tried to make motion, but couldn't ; tried to utter words, but failed.

Once, a whirling pillar of fire wreathed itself around him within which he saw a glittering nucleus of a jewelled eye that fixed on him, unblinkingly, from all sides, until the heat and light it emitted , laser-like, were simply too much to endure.

Help me, his lips formed the words, but not a sound escaped his lips.

Next, a procession of indescribable beasts marched past him, big and small, wild and tame, all stopping to silently look at him as they filed past.

One moment he was lying gently on the heather, in a field of waving flowers; another, he was hopping over live hot coals, screaming in agony.

Great big birds came swooping down , from the sky, noisily flapping outsize wings, missing him by mere inches in their screaming, bullet-like, predatorial dives.

Sunamis he could see, from hundreds of yards away, slowly advanced toward him, submerging him repeatedly in their terrifying depths, and he still could not untether himself from that vintage tree.

How much time had passed by, he could hardly know or feel.

He could not tell whether he was dead or alive.

He felt reduced to a bare point of flickering light at the far end of a long, dark tunnel.

CHAPTER ONE HUNDRED AND TWENTY
Visions

There are dreams from which we cannot wake.

Others from which we must not wake.

Still others, where we cannot decipher whether we are asleep or awake.

He was in that latter state.

Where he was, he didn't know.

Who he was, he didn't know.

All had become but a single point of concentration, that denied itself, and floated, hither and thither, like a bobbing pin in a shaken bowl of liquid.

He noticed nothing, heard nothing, felt nothing.

Yet he was not dead, but in a state of perfect rest, in a sort of arrested animation.

The world and he just merged into a oneness that denied separateness.

He floated, weightless, on the vast ocean of cosmic consciousness that we call life.

He was, or felt, immune: to all earthly ills.

Raging forest fires swept perilously past him, leaving him untouched and unscathed.

Violent storms buffeted the swaying tree, but not a hair on his head moved.

Despite his apparent immunity, the universe yet appeared to test him, fearfully, in every conceivable way.

Images of food, and concupiscent corpulence, danced before

him in games of dark allegory and temptation.

But he was in another, rarefied ether, where mortal vanities could not subsist.

It is the Egoless world.

The world without want, or desire.

The only world where Man can be free of his own innate, and dire, propensity for evil.

A world given, and available, to all.

A world that leaves even god impotent.

CHAPTER ONE HUNDRED AND TWENTY-ONE
Ego

The *Journey to the Center of the Ego* is, usually, a perennial one.

What lies beyond that long tunnel of biochemical self-saturation, we cannot be sure.

But we can know this: once commenced, this journey may not be terminated at will - other forces we cannot hope to fathom take over that limit the autonomy of the soul.

He was on just such a journey; indeed, had been so since childhood, though with little self-awareness.

The universe, as a principle, seems to discourage such voyages: they seem to interfere with nature's obscure plans for sentient beings.

On the other hand, a few appear perhaps unduly chosen to be granted such form of temptation.

Some are given glimpses into the riddles of eternity, tantalising visions that never amount to a comprehensible tale, either because of the indecipherable nature of things, or because of our limited, human, capacities for cognition.

Out of such narrow intimations, the human mind weaves, perhaps necessarily large tales, deep confabulations.

As he sat motionless, the struggle between such inexplicable intuitions began in earnest.

He was visited by dreams that devoured his senses, yet left no coherent, or lasting, impression.

Others, whom he had forgotten or left behind, family, friends, passing acquaintances, returned in life-like form, and stood like still sentinels beside him.

Yet, they said nothing

He dreamed also of himself dreaming - laughing, crying, plunged in the depths of despair, or exulting with some rare, ineffable, elation.

He could, at times, see himself squatting under the tree, as if he were an apparition high above gazing down at the world.

Other times he was inside of himself, like a lone atom, swimming up his own , restless, swirling, bloodstream.

CHAPTER ONE HUNDRED AND TWENTY-TWO
Samadhi

One day, or it may have been night, the visions stopped.

There was absolutely nothing.

No sound.

No movement.

No color.

All had blended into One.

Into stillness.

The internal, the external, were all fused.

In that timeless, formless, motionless ,Void - he sat frozen.

It was over.

His ego had perished - melted into what the sages of yore called *shunya,* the silence of the void.

A state of what, in popular mystical parlance, is referred to as *samadhi.*

It is., perhaps, what the unenlightened call enlightenment.

CHAPTER ONE HUNDRED AND TWENTY-THREE
Fusion

When he came to, life, color , and sound, returned - in separate, and variable, doses.

Birds chirped , nearabouts.

Coyotes howled, in the distance.

And the clouds above rolled, furled, and thundered.

He felt himself rising like Triton from the sea, in vertical motion, straight as an arrow.

He then descended slowly, as if he were walking down a steep, treacherous, staircase of air.

He now moved as if in soft billows, as mountains, valleys, and meadows, all seemed to glide by without any expense of effort.

He needed neither food nor drink.

Even his breathing was barely minimal, just enough, possibly, to sustain life.

His eyes were fixed far ahead of him, on the far horizon, as if unable to focus on more proximate vistas.

As he approached human habitation, the odd hiker passed him by with a quizzical, even apprehensive, glance.

The austerity of his motion, and his general aspect, was a sight that commanded attention.

But he wasn't looking for any.

Nor would he have noticed, had it come his way.

He was now one of mind, heart and resolve, yet devoid of each.

CHAPTER ONE HUNDRED AND TWENTY-FOUR
Absence of Vanity

The death of the ego is no ordinary demise.

It is like having no inside.

Being hollow, yet still quite full.

It is indescribable.

It has many implications.

But quite the strongest is the absence of vanity.

There is simply no further standard for evaluation.

No one is better, or worse, any more.

Nothing is craved, or desired.

It is a null state of Non-Discontent, without contrast.

Fear and hostility are equally absent.

All that prevails is a sort of a general. almost neutral, *Empathy*
that philosophers, and poets, waxing romantic, call love.

Without the ego, we blend, fade, into everything and become
nothing.

He was now, afoot, or aloft, on some, unscalable, predestined, wanderings.

One might say he was like a Siddhartha, but of the New
Millennium.

CHAPTER ONE HUNDRED AND TWENTY-FIVE
Voyaging

He had neither identification nor money on him.

But he travelled.

Sometimes people, usually younger people, gave him a ride, despite his strange appearance.

Occasionally, he stepped into a train - and, oddly enough, no conductor ever seemed to notice him enough to ask him for his ticket, or a fare.

It was the same in buses.

Once, he found an abandoned bicycle, and rode it for days.

He stopped always at public gatherings, or just gatherings of people, and listened.

He seemed to hear the same reprise everywhere.

The world appeared united now- if only in fear and distrust.

At one street corner, he saw a television screen in an electronics store.

He saw his wife, on the screen, making an impassioned speech rallying people to march on Washington.

The audience, revealed in a quick cameo now and then, showed no sign of his son.

Every so, a policeman would come up beside him, and ask him to move on.

Children followed him for a while, laughing and teasing, before giving up.

He ate little, save what was given him as alms by some kindly restaurateur.

He slept under bridges, in tunnels, and in parks.

His attire depended on the generosity of thrift-store owners, who parted with an odd garment or two - without solicitation. He washed in streams, ponds, and in public washrooms.

Every evening, he stood in silence- watching the sun go down, all the way from dusk, sunset, twilight, and into night.

Every morning, he greeted sunrise with mental ablutions, moist of heart and eyes.

Though he was not self-aware, since he had no self, he had to see it all - before it was, all of it, all too soon, taken away.

CHAPTER ONE HUNDRED AND TWENTY-SIX
Nightfall

He stood by the sea, under a moonlit sky.

The wind buffeted the bobbing waves , which lapped noisily on the shore.

Tender is the night, he recited, and haply the queen moon is on her throne surrounded by all her starry fays.

The sea seemed to signify the Beginning - and the End.

He strolled into it, until submerged ,up to his waist.

But the currents did not pull or tug at him - but left him there, all but unmoving.

Neither the beginning nor the end are ours to choose, he echoed deep inside.

He stepped back out on the beach, and lay on the sand , looking up to the stars.

They all seemed to wink at him, as if they all knew , and shared, a private joke.

The firmament. How heavenly it could look!

What a splendidly resplendent universe, if other things on earth were in place.

But they almost never were.

And so the dismal Saga went on.

Struggle, strife, and then: all this gratuitously lavish beauty.

What a waste it was, the beauty that is.

Why create beauty, and infest it with such rank violence?

A dog-eat-dog world of endless, gratuitous, splendor.

Too paradoxical: but, for now, his eyes rested in peace on it all.

It was god's Plan.

He was not going to offer critique.

What was the point?

CHAPTER ONE HUNDRED AND TWENTY-SEVEN
War

He passed by soldiers marching off to war.

What a bizarre sight it was.

Young men, walking in unison, to the sound of a tribal drum beat.

Young men from all round the world were doing the same.

Everywhere, the pious, much as the hypocritical, invoked god to protect them - and quell the enemy.

Surely, there is no end to human stupidity.

Why did sons listen to their fathers?

Why did men die for their country, when no country would die for them?

It was profoundly irrational, and yet stirring.

People threw garlands at them as if they were heroes already, lomg before they had taken to the field.

How we love to cheer on others to certain martyrdom!

Makes us feel warm and fuzzy inside, perhaps, until the coffins come home, darkly draped , in flags.

Then, it's all solemnity, and shame.

Too late.

CHAPTER ONE HUNDRED AND TWENTY-EIGHT
Words

He passed by great government orators who told restless crowds that light was come gleaming , through the far end of the tunnel (blight might have been a more accurate word!).

That the on-going War could be won.

That they could survive a Nuclear war, with but elementary precautions.

That Peace was at hand.

That the Enemy was to blame, for all the mayhem in the world.

That only a few bad apples were at fault.

And so on.

And the words fell like balm to some, manna to others – and just galled others.

But they were only Words.

Ordinary people paid way too much attention to them.

It was simply the way with them.

CHAPTER ONE HUNDRED AND TWENTY-NINE
Fractures

He passed by looters, and arsonists, that were exploiting the general breakdown.

Police, who looked the other way.

Offices, that were shut down.

Businesses, that had shuttered up.

He passed by children that played on in the streets, regardless.

And the endless processions of cars and trucks, leaving the cities, heading for the country.

Pets, let go by their owners, roamed the streets playfully, unaware of the catastrophe around.

Hydrants left running soaked rotting garbage mounding up high at the corners of city blocks.

Chic bars were brightly lit, nonetheless, and loud music played at the corner pubs.

Is this the way the world ends, he thought?

Give everyone a fiddle, and a tankard of ale, why not, as we watch it all go ablaze?

We know not what we do, nor why we do it.

Only women, children, and puppies , go about the world infused with summary, immanent, viable, *Purpose.*

CHAPTER ONE HUNDRED AND THIRTY
Nausea

Nausea.

It could not touch him now, now that he had risen from the ghost of his past.

But he could see it clearly envelop the land, and its people, like a miasma.

The bondings were being broken, ties severed.

And next came the joyless sequestering, each from all.

Each cut loose, adrift, unable to Connect.

How he might have loved to rush away from them all.

The toadies, the humbugs, the Others.

Yet, he was not really rushing.

There would have been no point to it.

He himself was but a singular point in motion.

And the motion was the desideratum, and the dimension.

All else was without Meaning.

But the all else was spinning around him like a whirlwind gone wild.

CHAPTER ONE HUNDRED AND THIRTY-ONE

Senescence

Senescence, decay.

Dry rot, and wet rot.

Flotsam and jetsam.

Dismemberment, and death.

The Sordid was mixing with the Sublime.

There was nothing left to feel.

The invasion of the soul-snatchers had been supremely successful.

Bare bodies, empty souls.

The self-exalting species was sinking fast.

Man, the Last Perversion.

And the planet was , most triflingly, casting off its one hundred thousand year yoke.

Without so much as a tear.

If only They Knew.

CHAPTER ONE HUNDRED AND THIRTY-TWO
Playing Dice

The planet had no gender, ethnicity.

Nor did it care.

Like god, it operated according to certain statutory principles.

And nothing outside its perennial orbit really mattered.

It did not infuse its denizens with significance.

Pitiless, and Non-Anthropic, like the larger universe we inhabit.

True, men did it to themselves - and others.

Killed, maimed, and burnt.

Children, women, and lesser species perished, suffered perennially.

But *It* took no notice.

Bombs had fallen before, but the heavens did not cry out.

The slaughter fields stretch endlessly from the past to the present, and furl on to the extinguishing future.

God was always playing dice, with creation, drunk with Its own self-glory.

It makes the rules, but doesn't really play the game in good faith.

CHAPTER ONE HUNDRED AND THIRTY-THREE
Text, and Context

As he flitted, absorbing visions of the Cataclysm, he realized his own emancipation was devoid of any real meaning.

Others may abide the question, but he was free.

Yet there was no real import to it.

There was no Other, apparently, to situate it.

There could be no text, without context.

No tale, without an audience.

It was like solving the riddle of the Sphinx: and having only the Sphinx to tell it to.

CHAPTER ONE HUNDRED AND THIRTY-FOUR

Tides

He sat on the crag of a cliff, looking out to sea.

The eternal sea.

It would still be there, after submerging all else within its heaving, fulsome, darkness.

The sea was the repository of our collective deaths.

The early rays of dawn streaked across its surface, like lasers , illuminating every turn of wave, and catching each crest with a searing dapple of light.

How torturously beautiful creation could be, despite its seamless cruelty.

But, most humans needed a full belly to notice it, and maybe not even then.

The empty bellies felt it, too, but only as a Sonata of Pain.

He felt, though seated, as if he were soaring across the ocean like a racing rocket.

Beneath, the tide rose and the tide fell.

CHAPTER ONE HUNDRED AND THIRTY-FIVE
Choice

He had now circumnavigated the contours of his own consciousness.

Moved toward, and away, but always equidistant, from the center of his own existence.

He was now within, and without, the universe.

To what end?

It was unclear.

As unclear as the existence he had left behind.

None of us know who we are, why we are here.

But he had transcended the question, not answered it.

A sort of a karmic escape – from karma.

That much is available to each of us.

Exile is worth it, but only if the kingdom repels.

Thus far, he had been chosen: now he was doing the choosing.

So as not to choose at all.

CHAPTER ONE HUNDRED AND THIRTY-SIX
Materialism

His travels were not intended to bear fruit.

Indeed, it was unclear to him whether he was truly traveling , materially, at all.

Maybe he was still under that tree in the canyons, ruminating.

Or. maybe, some part of him was.

There was no telling.

In the pure ether of that state of consciousness, materiality is quite immaterial.

Time may have been passing, or standing still, he could not tell.

But he was wrapped up in motion of some kind.

Where he would arrive was unknown.

As yet.

CHAPTER ONE HUNDRED AND THIRTY-SEVEN
Serfdoms

Sunsets came and went, and so did the rains.

He could not be sure where he was.

But he was, yet again, far from people.

From their daily concerns.

From the turbulence of normalcy.

From the slavery of routine.

From the serfdom of habit.

Love and hate had become as one.

Neither existed, because of ego-death.

There was a Panacea for you!

Let the ego die, and there is no more cause for War, even internal war.

CHAPTER ONE HUNDRED AND THIRTY-EIGHT
Quest

Ego-death.

That was the key.

That was his Quest, and his Wandering.

But he had found it, oddly, long before he went seeking.

There was no necessity for a Grand Quest.

The mission was accomplished before even begun.

Exile and kingdom were now the same, like pain and pleasure fusing at some distal point of ecstasy.

He was delivered.

He was saved.

He was no more.

BOOK FOUR:

NATIVITY

CHAPTER ONE HUNDRED AND THIRTY-NINE
Return

The wicket gate by the farmyard creaked, as he swung it.

It was eventide, and the lamp on the porch burnt low.

He walked slowly up the path to the patio.

He paused at the door, then pushed the door ajar.

He could see his wife in the kitchen.

She affected no surprise in seeing him.

His son went running past him, followed by the dog.

It was all restored.

This was not the Day After, nor Yesterday.

It was the Present.

The present, which would imminently end in catastrophe - forever.

He sat by the kitchen table.

Had a long day?, asked his wife.

He looked at her, but said nothing.

Dinner will be ready soon, she said.

CHAPTER ONE HUNDRED AND FORTY
The Tale

In bed, she told him she had to be leaving the next day.

You couldn't stay, he asked?

What for?, she answered.

She had, apparently, no memory of all that he had, recently, shared with her, after his return from the future.

He could try telling her the tale all over again.

But it would seem too incredible.

Almost seemed that way, even to him.

He held her close that night, closer than was normal.

What is wrong? She asked.

Nothing, he said.

CHAPTER ONE HUNDRED AND FORTY-ONE
Morning

The next morning dawned, bright and gay.

It was summer, and all the world outside was duly festive.

Birds twittered, breezes blew softly, and trees swayed about as if drunk with the embalming warmth.

He sat by his equipment in the front yard, as the dog raced about worrying twigs.

He saw his son canter by, trying to fly a kite.

Soon, his wife came out, all dressed up in a prim business suit.

Off to New York, she said., my ride will be here soon.

He looked at her.

Heard the news?, she asked.

He nodded, in the negative.

Japan has now declared war on China.

Oh, he said.

What's the world coming to?, she asked rhetorically.

Armageddon? he inquired, wryly.

She looked at him.

There's an emergency session at the UN.

He grimaced.

A car horn tooted.

He looked up.

It was that man again.

The man in the car waved.

She walked up to bus him on the cheek, prior to leaving.

G'bye, she said, wish us all luck.

Luck, he asked?

We need it: if we can't get the Security Council to act, we're all dead.

He looked at her, and the man who had now stepped out the car.

We are all dead anyhow, he said, softly.

She shook her head, and with an unhappy look back at him, got in the car.

The gears crashed noisily, as the car accelerated.

CHAPTER ONE HUNDRED AND FORTY-TWO
The Daze

He parked the tractor in the shed.

He didn't much feel like farm labors today.

He sought his son, but couldn't readily find him, so he sat on the trunk of a fallen tree and fell into a reverie.

The brilliance of the day was almost too lavish to bear.

The sun poured on like malted honey, and the midsummer daze had taken possession of all farm animals.

By the calendar, it was but Three Days to Apocalypse.

And, all he was doing was listening to the bees buzz around the flower beds.

He could sketch every minute of what was to come.

She would return from New York, and leave again that Last Day.

And his son...

He rose from his perch on the tree stump.

There must be something he can do.

By force of habit, he walked toward the glen where he always went, when overcast with doubt or despair.

Today, he was moved by neither.

It was merely to deliberate a course of action.

CHAPTER ONE HUNDRED AND FORTY-THREE
Mirrors

The little cathedral in wood stood fast by the glimmering pond , with its mirror-like surface.

The gentle rays of the mid-morning sun filtered through the leaves like benediction.

He stood by the edge of the pool, where minor ripples broke the even surface of the pond in playful reprise.

He dropped to his knees.

There was nothing he could do.

The gods had forsaken the world.

Men had gone but the way of men.

He could neither rouse the millions, nor the few, to reverse the tide. That much, he simply knew.

Even as he knelt, blind men in boardrooms were preparing to push the fateful buttons that would end an entire phase of evolution.

He found it hard to form words of prayer.

His lips just would not move.

What a fit place to die, he thought, surrounded by such ethereal, unspeakable beauty.

But his own fate was far worse than death, he remembered.

He was destined to outlive all.

God was punishing him more severely than the rest.

Besides, he had to be there for his little boy until.... .

His death lay in knowing, watching, and most awful fate of all: surviving the world.

Even tears were not to be a respite.

Immortality is not a boon, if given but to One.

CHAPTER ONE HUNDRED AND FORTY-FOUR

Scripts

There are tragedies that are inexorable.

There are tragedies that are preventable.

There are tragedies that are curable.

His was beyond description

It was beyond belief.

It was beyond comprehension.

He could seek no solace from anyone, or anything.

There was nothing at all redeemable.

He had to follow the script to the bitter end, without volition.

Why him?

Of the seven billion on the good earth.

There were no answers, only imperatives.

On his knees still, he slipped into a reverie, head bowed deep and resting upon his knees.

Almost imperceptibly, he slowly keeled over - right into the pond.

CHAPTER ONE HUNDRED AND FORTY-FIVE
The Pool

In that statuesque pose, he went straight down to the bottom, unmoving.

On the floor bed of the pond, he came to rest, still in a sitting stance.

He opened his eyes to see blazing crystals all around him beaming their lights straight upon him.

Dazzled, he closed his eyes, but could still see the glistening, moist, vista about him.

The crystals, in great ornate shapes and sizes, surrounded him in a great wide circle, each with a pincer-like beam that flashed straight upon his face.

He was, in effect, at the center of a great energy field.

Possibly, it was like being at the epicenter of a nuclear reaction.

Why he had not drowned, he didn't care to interrogate.

He was not breathing at all. He kept his eyes closed.

If this were death, it was premature. He still had days left.

The lights beamed not merely upon him, but penetrated within. It was like a great one-way energy transfer.

He could interpret the intense beams of light into words that flashed out like little shining stars, in the great receptacle of his open mind. The words arranged themselves into structured morphemes of Meaning.

The Great Light was speaking, so to speak, and he could receive, if but in the airy language of beams.

CHAPTER ONE HUNDRED AND FORTY-SIX
A Void

He opened his eyes, and withstood the lasers.

Go ahead, said the beams, invent me.

Why?, he asked.

Because you have need of me.

I do not need you, he said.

Then your world does, the world I showed you, and you alone, after the Great Rains.

I?

Yes, I.

Who are you?

Something waiting to be invented.

And why must I invent you: why not someone else?

There are others: to each, her own way.

Am I dead?

No.

Then where am I?

In the void, in between worlds.

I need to be back in mine.

I can't let you go: not until you invent me first.

And what then?

Then I can be the god you all seem to wish to have.

What use are you to anyone?

I can save your world, from your kind.

You can't.

Why not?

Because of the oddball will we seem to possess.

You don't have free will: that's just a necessary delusion.

Why necessary?

To preen your ego.

So it's a trick!

Yes.

Are you no more than a trickster?

I am nothing yet: you have to invent me first.

I don't know if I care to.

Don't you wish to save your son?

How do I invent you?

Just tell me the traits you want in me.

I don't know any.

Consult all those Scriptures you have floating about on your planet: they write of me as if I were their close brother-in-law.

You scorn your own believers!

I tire of them: they wish me to be too many things. It's not as if even I can create a round square, nor a stone too heavy to be lifted - by me.

What are you?

A dream.

Am I dreaming now?

You are always dreaming, the lot of you.

Do I exist?

As much as I do, and I am not even invented yet.

And this great big universe?

Make believe: I made believe.

Why?

To stay amused: it is lonely - not being invented yet.

You find great big whirling orbs of cataclysmic fire amusing?

That was experimental: it's not as if I got it right the first time.

And all the laws of nature?

Well, the project had to be kept going: I didn't wish to be employed all the time.

Are you just One?

Depends.

On what?

On what you wish me to be: I am many, I am one, I am none.

Why must the world die?

That wasn't my program: you folks blew it.

But the sun, it will burn out someday. So it was, all along, a Project of Doom.

Not necessarily: something else always comes along.

Is there a devil?

Yeah.

Really!

Sure: it's just me, in a bad mood.

A split personality.

Sort of.

Good grief.

So, what's it going to be: what awful form do you wish me to assume?

It doesn't matter.

What?

You don't matter.

Really?

Sure: we invented you – we can disinvent you.

But, then: where'd you be?

Exactly where I am, at the bottom of a pool talking to light beams.

You are lost, my boy.

Not as much as you.

Hey.

True, isn't it?: there is no point to the universe. To Me. To You. To Anything. So, whether you exist or not alters nothing. The lights deepened in brilliance, as the pool frothed and bubbled.

He felt himself passing out.

The lights converged on him, as he struggled to shade his eyes.

Stop, he shouted. Stop.

Who're you talking to, dad?, asked a little voice, wake up.

He hugged his little boy , who had ambled up, looking for him, with the dog.

He must have fallen asleep by the rocks.

He looked down at the pool.

It rippled slightly in the light breeze.

Light beams?

Not likely.

CHAPTER ONE HUNDRED AND FORTY-SEVEN
Meaning

He walked home, with his son straggling along thoughtfully.

It had seemed all too real.

And he never dreamt, usually, certainly not in the daytime.

The dog and his son cantered past him, each bouncier than the other.

He smiled.

The Meaning of Life.

Did he need any more of it?

So, what was he to do?

Nothing?

There were but days, indeed so many hours left.

He threw his head back – and laughed out loud.

The boy stopped.

What's so funny, dad?

Everything, he replied, you, me, the dog, the universe.

His son was not smiling.

I want mommy, he said.

He stopped, and sighed.

Yes, I know, he said.

Dear god.

CHAPTER ONE HUNDRED AND FORTY-EIGHT
The Self

That night, as his son slept, he sat up on the porch and looked up at the stars.

What would happen now?

Would it all go on as before?

Would the world end, in just two days?

Would everyone be gone again?

Would he be the sole survivor, trying to fight his way up the slopes just to breathe?

And where would they be, his wife, his son, their dog?

He looked up at the heavens.

The stars smiled back.

How deceptive the universe was!

We look up at night, and see a smiling, twinkling universe.

But it was a burning, raging, furious cascade of swirling infernos.

Maya.

What dupes we are.

So where would they all be, After the Crash?

He sat silent.

The moon, and the stars, became a blur.

He entered, yet again, that silent void of still consciousness.

It was a calm world, that.

And he saw that everything was there - and not there.

His heartbeat stabilized, and slowed down.

His breathing was almost non-existent.

Everything exists to give us meaning.

But, it is there only on account of its meaning.

So the universe was not about others, or even god.

It was about him.

The solitary Self.

The Void within.

All things do pass.

And then one day so would he, and the little void inside would merge into the larger void outside.

CHAPTER ONE HUNDRED AND FORTY-NINE
Letting Go

It was now almost early pre-dawn.

He sat still even now, as the heavens, alternately, changed hue.

He felt a dawn of, albeit dim, comprehension.

The point to it, is to accept the world as it is.

And let it go on, as it will.

There was no holding it, holding out, nor holding on.

We are temporary guests, ever ready to depart.

Love it or hate it, it didn't much matter.

Deep passions were misleading.

A good laugh, or a careles shrug, possibly, served one better.

Maya is the act of a Jester – and the universe is but a very poor Witticism.

Letting go, resignedly, or laughing the while, was perhaps the only sane human response to this Indefinability.

Struggle was pointless.

Asking for full disclosure, impossible.

We are all (fore) doomed – to a species of Trivial Extinction.

CHAPTER ONE HUNDRED AND FIFTY
Stardust

The day was dawning that would have him face the indefinable again.

He could scarce believe it.

History repeating itself, in divine tragi-comedy.

Yet, how can we , the victims, mock extinction?

What else is there to do?

Crying didn't seem to mend things, or dull the pain.

So, to grimace, and let go – *That was The Way*.

God was, apparently, a comic playwright: and we, the captive audience – except, the joke, sadly, was on us.

So, this time around, he had to still the caring; or , leastways,the display of it.

Everything in the universe is doomed: even the universe itself.

So, why worry?

Sooner,or later, we are all stardust.

There is no *dharma* other than the passive endurance of existence.

Sure, we could struggle, to steal this, or cap that: but that only made the gods surly and churlish.

Plus struggle seemed to waste us as a species anyway.

Life is struggle in itself: so why struggle just to live?

We were all Nowhere men and women: going nowhere, coming from nowhere, unsure whether we be coming or going.

But was there yet, a little joy – if but given to some.

He could savor the sunrise, and enjoy the warblings of his little boy.

He didn't need to struggle, for much – all had been given him that now would be, just as easily, taken away.

Everything was the same this time around, with one major *Caveat.*

His attitude.

That would have to change.

He knelt, as the sunrise stoked the farmyard with its cool, blanching heat.

Light was breaking everywhere, in roseate hues.

Dear god, he prayed, I know not what I must do: but why? Why?

CHAPTER ONE HUNDRED AND FIFTY-ONE
Dawning

The rubescent dawn now creased into unfolding day.

The dusty sunrise was now blanched by darkling light.

A sultry wind struck up to the south of the farmyard, and blew warmth and the light, or so he felt, through his hair.

He had fallen asleep on the porch.

It was the Day Before.

He awoke abruptly.

Soon, his son would wake and then, just as surely, the dog.

He looked up at the heavens.

They stretched high, and fair ,and blue, as ever.

No signs,whatsoever, there of impending doom.

The universe was about to waste a species, maybe the entire planet, but felt it inopportune to issue a warning.

He rose, and stepped into the hallway leading to his son's room.

The boy was asleep, smiling in his sleep.

Dreaming, obviously.

But wasn't it all a dream?

The dream of Life, the dream of Death, the dream of a Hereafter.

Next to his bed lay the dog, also lost to the world.

A mood-breaking crash of gears announced the arrival of his wife, let out of a limo by the tall man: he could see them from the open screen door.

She bustled in.

I am so glad to see you, she said.

He looked at her.

Are you?

She paused.

Yes, she said.

Why?

Why what?

Why are you glad to see me?

She gave him a hug.

Because, according to you, we are never to meet again.

I didn't say that, he said.

Close enough, she said.

He smiled at her.

She was, leastways to him, very beautiful.

Know what?

What?, he replied.

I think I believe you.

Better late than never, he said, but why?

She unfolded a newspaper banner.

Look, she said, we have declared war on Russia.

CHAPTER ONE HUNDRED AND FIFTY-TWO
Faith

They sat at the kitchen table, holding hands.

I love you, she said.

He smiled.

Oh, he said.

Tell me it's not true.

What.

The end of the world story.

He smiled again.

It is true.

Then why are you so darned cheerful?

Because, he said, I don't believe in anything, anymore.

What do you mean?

I don't believe in the world, in human nature, in you, in us, in anything.

She looked aghast.

But I can make believe I do, he said, that's what we all do. That's all we can do.

Are you telling me, on the day that is to be our last - that you don't care?

I didn't say that.

But...

I said I don't believe in our existence, in our temporality: I think all of it, the world is just delusion.

Delusion — we are at war: is that a delusion?

It is as real, as we are unreal.

There was silence. She looked at him closely. Tears welled in her eyes,

I've been unfaithful to you, she sobbed.

He said nothing, then burst out laughing.

She stopped crying, again aghast.

I am serious, she said.

I know: but I am not. There is no faith to be unfaithful to.

I slept with him.

He nodded.

Yes, he said, and it has no meaning.

It just sort of happened., of a sudden.

I know, he said softly, just like us.

She looked at him.

I did find him… attractive.

He said nothing.

Want to know why?

No.

Because he cared… about everything. He wanted to make a difference.

And I don't?

She said nothing.

He leaned forward.

And where will they all be, the Carers and the Non-Carers, just one day from now?

She looked at him.

We all end up in the same bed.

She kept silent.

You cry because you slept with him: I laugh because we all sleep together in the end, in the same earthly bed.

She averted her eyes.

So tell me, he said, were you seriously saving the world all these days: or busy , under its noble cover ,enraptured in this great, torrid romance of your new , ever so passionate, early mid-life?

Her lips quivered.

He placed a hand on her shoulder.

It's ok, my sweet. It really is. You see, it really doesn't matter.

Would it have mattered, if…

If the world were not about to end? No: because it has always been predestined to go, unreal like the rest of us, part of a defunct computer game left behind by an extinct programmer.

She looked into his eyes.

They were smiling.

We have neither beginning, a middle, nor an end: it's a perfect circle we traverse, day in and day out, lifetime after lifetime, illusion upon illusion.

She burst into tears.

I am so sorry, she cried.

He hugged her.

Me too, he said softly, but not for the same reasons.

CHAPTER ONE HUNDRED AND FIFTY-THREE
The Wake

They waited for their son to wake.

The rapture with which his wakening was greeted surprised the little boy.

It's not my birthday, is it, he asked?

No, said his father.

Then what?

Well, he answered, we are all going to be - going away.

Where?

I don't know.

Sounds like fun.

The father stayed quiet.

Let's have breakfast, said the mother.

Later, as the boy played in the yard, she turned to him.

What now?

It is scripted: you will leave to save the world, and I will stay home.

And then?

Poof, he said.

She bit her lip.

We are such stuff as dreams are made of.

I will not accept that, she said.

I know, he replied. That is scripted, too.

Maybe the world will end, but I must do what I must do.

Which is?

Go to D.C., and…

See your…friend… one last time?

No: for I am seeing him right now, she said, intently.

For one last time then, he replied, whispering, why must you leave?

What if I can get them to listen to you?

How?

B---- knows the President: went to Law School with him

B--?

Yes, she said, averting her eyes.

So that was his name.

They won't listen.

Will you speak to them, if I can get you the time?

There isn't enough time.

Leave it to me, she said, and I will return, You will be home.

And we will all be together.

He smiled.

The power of positive thinking?

The power of rationality , that cannot, will not, accept the irrational.

Is he a nice guy?, he asked after her, as she walked away.

CHAPTER ONE HUNDRED AND FIFTY-FOUR
Over the Hill

Suddenly, he remembered the mountain, and the climbing.

That was the power of rationality, and positive thinking.

It brought him back only to where he was, but after Herculean effort.

Now, he would approach it differently.

Son, he called out.

Yeah, dad?

Wanna go play ball?

Sure, dad.

And get some ice cream later?

Sounds swell, dad.

He smiled.

Some joys even the gods can't deny us.

CHAPTER ONE HUNDRED AND FIFTY-FIVE
Yearnings

He watched her leave, as he watched her once before.

She was a heroine, in an Unheroic world.

She hugged their son, and kissed him.

See you tomorrow, darling, she said.

Yes, mom, said the boy.

She waved, and blew him a kiss.

The car pulled up outside the gate.

He could see the dark silhouette of the man.

The car pulled away.

I love you, he whispered softly , after her.

He saw her turn back, with a smile, as if she had heard.

CHAPTER ONE HUNDRED AND FIFTY-SIX
Replay

The neighbors pulled in the driveway, as before, and left again as before.

It was all repeating itself.

He stepped out in the yard, and looked at the farmyard.

On impulse, he untethered all the animals and stood back, and watched as they scampered away, if somewhat diffidently.

It was a glorious morning, and the sun stood at the very apex of a lofty sky.

What a perfect day for a ball game.

Come on, son, he said, let's go play.

Wait dad, said the boy, can I bring Woof?

Sure, he said., why not? He loves ball games - and ice cream, too.

CHAPTER ONE HUNDRED AND FIFTY-SEVEN
Long Night

Sunset racked the horizon.

The dog and his son were licking at the same cone.

They were all disheveled, and unkempt , from the ball game, and the romping in the sun.

It would, if calendar held, be their Last Night together.

He looked at his son as only a father can: seeing more than just the boy.

His eyes welled up.

The sun, now dipped beyond the blue line, suddenly rent the scape with blinding iridescence.

It was a magnificent spectacle, though only a charade.

He thought of her, momentarily, as his son's face took on her visage.

Of a sudden, he blacked out, overpowered by strong emotion.

He fell limp to the ground, and then came to.

His son and the dog, way ahead, were quite unaware of his motions.

He rose to his knees, as the sun lingered on for a split second before suddenly plunging into the deep, below the far horizon.

Hands clasped, and shaking, he prayed to the irradiating twilight.

We believe, he whispered, because it is far too terrifying not to.

The heavens, dark as they were, merely smiled a sanguine smile, tinged with the lowering gloom of eventide.

There is neither beginning nor end, nor meaning: save what we invest the universe with, they seemed to be saying.

We invent it all, the cosmos, our existence, our gods.

There is nothing Within - or Without us.

And yet our Doubt, not our faith, keeps us believing, even unto the end.

For, sad to say, were there to be a god, it wouldn't really matter: a god that chose not to reveal its nature, its intent and its pleasure, to every living being, freely, openly, warmly, and unstintingly, and at all times - could only be a god quite worth ignoring.

CHAPTER ONE HUNDRED AND FIFTY-EIGHT
Crossing Lines

That night he imagined he had a dream, a very vivid, disturbing dream, but yet only a dream.

In it, he seemed to hear a voice saying:

You have come close, closer perhaps than others, but still not close enough.

He could not but understand now.

There was Nothing – to decipher.

So, there is no Crossing the Line.

Yet there might still be purpose to the Logos/Pathos of Creation: simply, perhaps, to question it, to the end, endlessly; instead of capitulating blindly, as with most, to the stark fear of the unknown; or, alternatively, rejecting Authorship of the universe, equally blindly; or even abstaining elegantly from reflection upon such issues.

Perhaps, a glimpse into the blank nothingness of reality is ultimately given, not to the pious supplicant, nor even the doubting skeptic, but to the undaunted Seeker of the Truth: though not altogether, and not all at once.

But Ignorance is far from the real tragedy: after all, even the sage Knower, high-blessed with 'enlightenment', like the Buddha, is laid to rest, in doubt – to rot.

Nor did even He - the Enlightened One- ever claim Omniscience. *Fourteen Questions, said he, to which there be No Answers.*

We are to question Why, Do - and then Die(still unknowing).

The last followed , even if one did nothing at all.

All paths are Not the Same, though they all led to the same pathetic end.

So, in a curious twist: Nothing *is* real.

Of course, it was only a dream, from which only he would wake.

Leastways, that's what he imagined he dreamt.

CHAPTER ONE HUNDRED AND FIFTY-NINE
Coda

The phone rang loudly, discordantly, jolting him awake.

He grabbed the receiver.

I finally got through, she cried, in great excitement, I am here with the National Security Advisor himself! Will you speak to him? He can get us on to the President.

It was 30 minutes to midnight. He was silent, for just a moment. Could it really be?

Hello, are you there?, She shouted.

Ask if he can have the President call off the ICBM launchings, he said slowly, right now: else, all is lost already.

But...

Ask him. Please.

He heard her speak.

A smooth male voice got on the line.

Can we speak?, it asked.

Afterwards, there's no time now; if you don't stop those launches, we'll all be extinct - before dawn.

I don't know what launches you're speaking of: but... I might be able to get you in with the President, if you explain to me what you know, and how you know it.

There is, he answered softly, no time for that: call off the missiles, right now. Seven and a half billion lives depend on it. Please.

There are no such plans: and even if there were, your request would still be quite impossible, as you must know.

I know that: I always knew that, he said, wanly, ok: can I just speak to my wife?

But, wait…

Please, it's very important. There really is no time.

She got back on.

He broke down, slowly sliding to the floor.

I am so sorry, he said, I didn't believe, or think you could really get anywhere. I thought…I didn't…I…

She spoke softly.

I love you, she said, and all I did, like I said… tried to do… all of it , was for us, too…

Memory shimmered , in shades of his boy asking what *he* was going to do about it all.

And what, dear heaven, *had* he done?

All too late , he wept, we did have…a very small chance!: how stupid…how purblind I've been…I was so sure that…if only…it's my own terrible, terrible, default: I was shown all, in hindsight and foresight.I am so very, very, sorry…

Hug junior for me, she murmured, crying now.

I… failed us all, he mumbled.

He heard her sob.

And Creation itself, he whispered, choking, closing his eyes.

The line went dead.

www.ingramcontent.com/pod-product-compliance
Lightning Source LLC
Chambersburg PA
CBHW031940010726
47493CB00007B/2010